THE PATRIOT'S DAUGHTER

KAMRYN GREEN
WITH
RICK GREEN

The Patriot's Daughter
© 2017 by Kamryn Green. All rights reserved.

For additional copies of this book or for more information on other books, contact:

Revolutionary Strategies
P.O. Box 900
Dripping Springs, TX 78620
(512)515-3744
www.RickGreen.com

Cover design:
KO Creative

Printed in the United States of America
ISBN 978-0-9981269-4-4

*"I can do all things through Him
Who strengthens me."*
- Philippians 4:13

To every boy and girl.
You can do all things through Him.

Acknowledgments

Dad—there's not a doubt in my mind that this book wouldn't be all that it is without you. Thank you for not only sticking by my side during this huge undertaking, but for never leaving my side no matter the dream I've wanted to pursue. You encourage continually, challenge patiently, and love unconditionally. When I've wanted to give up—you push me on. When I've been afraid of falling, you seek to lift me up, and reassure me again and again that the leap is worth it. How can I describe how much you mean to me? Thank you, Papa, for not only loving me so, but for daily pointing me back to the perfect love of our Father. That's the greatest gift a daughter could ever ask for.

Mom, Trey, Andra, Reagan, Rhett, and Arlin . . . I'm forever thankful for each one of you, your endless support, and every day that we get to spend laughing and learning together—a million hugs placed here.

Hannah—sister in Christ. Banana. Many more names that I probably shouldn't list cause' honestly, they're weird, let's admit it. Hannah Banana Macias. You are going to be acknowledged! The way you encourage and minister to me is the epitome of true friendship. I know that without your prayers, writing this book would have been very different. Thank you for always being there. I love ya.

Above all—Jesus. You dared my heart to trust Your faithfulness and dream like there's no tomorrow. Thank You that nothing is impossible with You.

Preface

I sat cross legged on my bed at thirteen years old, reading from my old Macbook that had a broken blue case. My dad sat in front of me and listened to the first chapter of a book idea I had—*The Patriot's Daughter*. It was little more than a concept, a story barely born with only two chapters at the time... but it was the start.

I cannot believe the first book to this series is now complete. Wow. The Lord is so good, because I admit to thinking many times that I'd never finish. When I first had the idea of *The Patriot's Daughter* almost four years ago, all I knew was that it would be about a young girl named Maddie Holt. This girl was searching for her purpose, for meaning in life.

I could relate.

Over the next three to four years, Maddie and I became best friends. I poured my heart into her, making her story a peek into my own life, what I've learned, and am still learning in all my seventeen years. It's been a wild ride with no true schedule. The only goal I had with this book was to have it published before I turned seventeen, which did happen, by the grace of God!

Through this story, I sincerely hope that you are engaged, challenged, and inspired. It is my passion and constant prayer that you hear the Lord speaking into your heart. Maybe you need to discover your purpose. Maybe you just need to know you have one—that you're so loved, that God

Almighty IS calling you, and that He has so much in store. If that is you, please read on.

I think you'll find that a fourteen-year-old girl named Maddie Holt is in the same place.

His,

Kamryn

River Springs, North Carolina

May 6, 1778

5 hours before the attack . . .

1
Chocolate and Chess

GREY AND WHITE COLOR THE SKY LIKE ASH.

Of course, it is just the clouds, but I like to think of them as proof of a wildfire in the heavens. My leather boots thump against wood, finding each stair in a familiar rhythm. My fingers wrap around the ends of my swooshing dress, gathering the material into a wrinkled ball . . .

Smack!

My body and solid wood collide, a grunt escaping through bitten down teeth. With a scrunch of my nose, my hands push off the porch.

Dumb dress.

I gather the material that escaped my fingers, snuck under my boot, and caused the trip. My petticoat is soft and light in my hands.

If only I could trade you for a pair of trousers.

Heat from the sun hits my neck, warm and welcoming, accompanied by a mouthwatering smell from *Annie's* wafting deliciously in the air. Flicking my auburn braid behind my shoulder, I hasten into the shop and am met by its owner and cashier.

Miss Annie Hays.

"Maddie!" A warm smile seems to shine in her entire face as bouncy, honeycomb colored curls drape over her shoulders and frame a soft jaw and rosy cheeks. As the only woman in this part of North Carolina to own and operate her very own business, no one can disagree that her heart is as strong as even the fiercest patriot soldier. Her husband was killed at the Battle of Brandywine, leaving the store in her possession.

Merchants from all around offered to buy, promising to leave a good fortune in her hands for the store, but she refused to sell, making a promise to keep the little shop open in honor of her husband. She's admired by many, her determination impressing even the colonel.

The colonel . . . Oh, Papa . . . how much longer before—

"What can I get for my favorite customer?" I turn, thoughts interrupted by the chipper voice. Miss Annie's mouth turns into a grin, soft and full lips protruding with a twinkle resting in her eye.

"Nothing out of the ordinary." I prop my elbows up on the finely smoothed counter, fists supporting my chin. Smirking mischievously, I reveal the secret behind my playful lips. "I snuck out." Seeing her smile disappear and the twinkle subside, I hurry—"It's only for a moment! She won't even know I am gone!"

"And does that make it right?" Her brow furrows in.

"Whoever said it was wrong in the first place?" I tilt my head, forehead raising. "She's not my mother, Miss Annie."

Her shoulders slump as she relinquishes from the argument and clicks her tongue. "Your wit is going to get you in trouble someday, Maddie dear."

I lightly smile, turning to the side. Hundreds of candies from Bakers Chocolate of Boston fill a wooden barrel. Chocolate sticks, blocks, and coco powder. Running the tips of my fingers along the paper-covered sweets, I wonder at Annie's resourcefulness since she is the only one in this part of the Carolinas that has treats so rare. Rumor has it that one of the Baker boys was saved by Annie's husband at Brandywine, and the Baker family now supplies the new candies as a way of saying thanks.

I pluck one chocolate stick from the bowl. "It's just, it's so hard to be around her, you know?"

"Maddie, you know she loves you—"

"Does she?" Years of irritation threaten to boil to the surface. I force my tone to soften, eyes fluttering with faint blinks as they stare into hers. "Miss Annie, I often find that hard to believe." She swallows, glancing at the counter in silence as I finger the paper in my hand. I sniff, slipping a hand back into my pocket to retrieve the pouch resting inside. "How's Lydia?" I pull out the pouch, turning it upside down so that various coins spill out with a *thump! thump! thump!*

"She's well."

My tone is absent, just hardly there as I place the chocolate stick on the counter with the coins. "I'm glad."

The well-trained side of her cashier voice comes back, but her eyes say something else — soft brown and glazed with sympathy. "Will that be all?"

"Just this." My shoulders lift with a shrug, lips pressing together tight. "Please."

She slides the coins into her palm. "Maddie." Her face softens, arms resting on the countertop. "You are so very dear to me. I hate to see you go through these feelings of enmity towards Sarah. Your father needed someone to look after you and Michael and she came along at just the right time."

I almost argue, ready to protest that it shouldn't have happened the way it did, that Papa didn't have to accommodate Sarah and her nettlesome daughter.

But what would it change?

She hands me the candy. "Please let me know how I can help. What you're feeling will not last forever."

My eyes flutter under the arch of my brow, fingers wrapping around the scratchy paper covering the chocolate. I force my eyes to look into hers, hating the uneasy feeling in my stomach. Clearing my throat, I grab the pouch. "Have a good day, Miss Annie." I turn on my heel, shooting back a glance and nodding politely as a farewell.

The bright spring sun nearly blinds me as I step out of the door. I mindlessly step off the porch, bundling my dress once again into a scrunched-up ball with one hand, stuffing the chocolate in my pocket. I take a few steps into the street, only to retreat just quickly enough to dodge an oncoming wagon. Horse's hooves stomp violently along with each lash of a whip, carrying the wagon by at an increasing speed.

That's strange. Normally it isn't ever this busy . . . must be new visitors.

Being far away from the larger cities has perhaps actually been in our favor, our lack of luxury helping to keep the fighting far from our small town.

"Whoa!" I veer out of the way, dodging a small boy dashing by. "Watch out young man!" He shoots back a smile and waves his hand, turning back just in time to sidestep the railing in front of Miss Annie's shop.

I continue walking along the side of the street, allowing myself to smile at the energy boiling over in the children all over town. A handful of kids dash past me, giggling to themselves and wondering happily about with their parents nearby. Perhaps it's natural for the little ones to become restless with so many fathers away at war. The people of town do not reject the playfulness of youth, rather gladly welcoming it into the atmosphere. Their laughter makes things better. Less gloomy. Less dreadful. It is much needed during a time such as this, when war has broken out all over the country. As one paper quoted Papa after the British massacred the local minutemen at Lexington, "The Sword is now drawn, and God only knows when it will be sheathed."

The thirteen colonies have indeed come together and fought hard, but Papa believes there are still worse days ahead for us.

I cross the street and make my way to the wood shop, walking up steps and through the ornately crafted door, my ears tuning in to the loud commotion coming from inside. At the thought of the old man's awaiting presence, I can't keep from smiling. "Uncle Henry? Hello?" I bang my fist against the doorframe, attempting to be heard over the tools scraping along wood.

No response.

I take a few steps more into the shop, placing my pouch with the last of my coins on a dark wooden table—a place that has become a favorite to spend time. Littered across the table are carefully carved figures, unrecognizable to practically every citizen of River Springs except Uncle Henry and myself. The table rests in-between a pair of rocking chairs, which sway gently from the breeze sweeping through the door, squeaking softly with each rock.

Peeking around the corner of a wall, I spot the elderly man working on some form of woodwork, planing back and forth, back and forth, then swiping the surface with a flick of his aging hand to rid the plank of any dust. Dressed in his leather apron, his skin is covered in a fine layer of saw dust.

"Uncle Henry?"

A smile lights his face as he glances up from his work. He beckons me over with his hand, mumbling a quiet but enthusiastic greeting. "Maddie! Come in, please, please."

I step forward into the room filled with every kind of tool imaginable, coughing momentarily at the fine dust floating in the air. "Th—thank—" My hand fans at the dust traveling around my nose. I catch my breath, holding back a sneeze. "Thank you, Uncle Henry." He smiles at my reply as enough dust finally disperses for me to speak. "I came for that special order I placed awhile back. Am I too soon?"

"No, no. In fact, it's been ready for the last few days, mhmm. The last few days." He glances at the ground hesitantly as if to search for something he might have dropped on the ground, though he never bends down to retrieve it.

I look about the compact room with eager eyes. "May I see?"

"Yes, yes, of course." His feeble legs carry him to the opposite side of the room from where I stand. He opens several drawers before finding the one he wants and rummages through it's contents.

I attempt to see what lies inside, rising on my tiptoes and straining my neck.

After a few moments of rustling around in the draw, he pulls out a wooden object, small and almost swallowed in his wrinkled fist. Walking back over, he places it in my hand as I accept the little figure. "I placed your payment on the table where we've been having our chess matches." My eyes catch the present.

"Oh, Uncle Henry!"

I glance into his gray eyes, smiling. "It's perfect. He's going to love it."

He nods. "It's one of my finest pieces of work." He studies the item as I run it over in my hand in fascination.

"It *is* exquisite." My fingers trace the detailed craftsmanship.

His lips press together in thought. The warmth in his gaze grows to be brighter, the fine lines around his mouth showing prominently as the corners of his lips turn up into a grin. "It is unique because of whom it is made for."

My face softens, and I move closer into his loving embrace, comforted by the simple warmth of his hug. He may not be my real uncle, but he's always been there, especially when Papa is gone. For that I am grateful.

"I better get going. Sarah will be looking for me." My right hand rests on his shoulder, eyes peering into his. "Thank you, Uncle Henry."

He lets out a mumble just loud enough for me to hear. "Anytime, anytime. Don't be shy about coming to visit me now. It's time I teach you a little trick with the Pawn known as *En Passant*!"

"I'll be back before you know it!" I give a playful wink and nod, vacating the room.

Uncle Henry is the only one in town that plays chess. He chose me to be his one student, often helping me pass the afternoons as I count the days until Papa's return. I've had to be creative with reasons to come downtown for lessons, since *some* people believe it to be a waste of time on a foolish game.

But Uncle Henry was right, it's undoubtedly made my mind sharper.

As I step out of the door, humid air blows on my skin, though not much hotter than it was inside the wood shop. I walk beside the street, my dress gathered into a ball for the third time. "Heaven help me if I don't ever find a way to avoid wearing you." I gather the material even more, letting my eyes linger on several young women nearby.

They sit under the shade of a shop's roof, most likely gossiping over the mundane news of the town. I glance down at my wrinkled dress. It's not that I despise my plain attire. In fact, I prefer it over their hats with colorful strings and dresses with bows and lace. It's that exploring as I do throughout the forest would be impossible in a frilly dress! If it wasn't for Sarah's dismissive attitude towards my wardrobe, I'd be dressed like the others. Lucky for me, she pays no attention to my clothing, or anything else about me.

I wonder to myself what life would be like if I had the luxuries of those in richer settlements or even of these women nearby sipping on their refreshments and nibbling on delectable treats.

How different would I be?

A breeze finds its way around the ends of my dress, warmed by the summer sun. Laughter floats in the air, boots and different styled shoes sounding a rhythmic shuffle along wooden walkways.

I wouldn't be myself, that much I know.

I have much time to think about these things when Papa is gone. Today marks three months and fourteen days, and still no sign of him or his troops. Some wouldn't give it much thought, being that he's a colonel, and his unique regiment is on active duty longer than others. But what has his regiment been doing these past winter months while most other soldiers are hunkered down, including General Washington and his men at Valley Forge?

Where could Papa be? Winter broke weeks ago and it has been unusually warm for May in Carolina.

I can't help thinking of the horrible possibilities. Is he alive? Is he on his way back with a wound? Or being held hostage in the darkest depths of one of the British's camps?

I wish I knew the answers to these questions, but I don't. Only when these long months of separation are over will I know. And when they are, my days will once again be filled with conversations by a fire.

I'll listen intently, knees huddled to my chest, eyes eagerly laid on his animated hand gestures as he retells his time away through stories. Stories of the countless battles. Stories of his men traveling throughout the vast forests of North Carolina, placing fear in the enemy's heart with their effective weapons and valiant acts. My favorite stories are the suspenseful ones, when he retells of leading his men through impossible odds, outnumbered and out-gunned by the superior and more experienced British forces.

The tales are invigorating. They carry spirit and life, stoking the burning sensation inside of me that I dare not share with a soul.

I want to be there with him.

In the thick of it all. In the grime and the victories of those battles Papa recounts with such pride, in the very middle of the smoke rising from muskets being fired all around. And I want to hear things, like my heartbeat quickening as a rush of energy spreads like a wildfire because a bullet just whizzed by my ear.

I want to live the story, not just hear it, and fight for the worthy cause called independence.

But, of course, there are other feelings. Those that I wish not to feel. During this time when he is absent, during this time that I wait and wait, this time is restless and the hours are long. For weeks at a time, I wonder where he is, whether he's safely studying maps and charts, or staring into the eyes of a malicious Red Coat as a weapon is aimed at his chest. Days drag on, convincing me that things will never get better until he's home.

When he is, however, wearing a grin like always, everything in my world is alright.

I shake my head slightly to myself, deciding to focus back on the life around me here and now, on the busy noises echoing off each porch chair and every shop sign. My head turns to look back at the center of town, the sounds of activity fading as I walk closer to home. I don't even need to look ahead to remember that a small house sits a hundred yards away, guarded by a cluster of surrounding trees, where unavoidable conflict awaits inside.

2

Storm Away

"WHAT KEPT YOU FOR so long?"

Sarah's slim frame enters the small room connecting to our kitchen. As her voice rings out, all that is heard is demand and anger. She grabs a rag to wipe gathering dust off of our aging furniture, unkempt hair pulled back into a bun. "You know that I need you here in the kitchen, not dallying about outside."

My shoulders slightly slouch against the back of our hard kitchen chair, eyes scaling the wall in front of me. "I'm sorry. Guess I lost track of time." I silently plead with God for this to not turn into another war of words. Remembering to respect Sarah as my elder and yet trying to hide my contempt for her feels almost impossible.

I slide out of my chair, a soft whistle from our teakettle beckoning me over. It rests on the cast iron stove, it's rusting handle jiggling slightly at the water boiling inside. Grabbing a rag, I wrap the handle and gently lift the teakettle off of the stove top.

"It's every day that you come home late," I hear a click from Sarah's tongue, "just as dinner is supposed to be getting ready. When will it stop, Maddie?"

I hold my breath, thinking of how to respond, but her clamorous mouth lets loose again before I can speak.

"Irene!" Sounds of her sorting through shelves reverberate off the kitchen walls. "I need you to run into town this evening. We're out of flour."

Steam from scorching water coats my skin in a thin, moist layer, escaping through the top of the teakettle as I delight in the opportunity to escape Sarah and go back into town. "I'll go. Irene is outside anyway." I peer into the dresser a few inches above my head, reaching inside to retrieve a cup. "As soon as I have my tea, I can—"

"Irene will go," her voice peaks, scornful. "You have already been to town today, and Irene needs to make her social circles far more than you do."

I turn to face her, fighting to stay composed. "I don't care about social circles. I'm just much faster at getting things done."

"You're staying, Maddie."

I start incredulously before thinking, "Why does it matter to you whether I go or Irene, as long as you get some flour?"

Her sparse brows raise in disapproval. "Do not question me!"

I bite my lip till blood meets my taste buds, fixing my attention back on the teakettle. Grabbing it's handle, my nerves tingle in annoyance. I tilt the spout downwards, a small flow of water pouring out, crystal clear water now light brown in color. The sudden sound of commotion makes my shoulders jump, a pair of boots shuffling and a boyish voice squealing in playful banter. Sarah gasps with a start, turning her head towards the direction of the noise.

"Michael Holt! If you dare to make any further ruckus for one more second, so help me, I will come in there myself to silence it!"

My eyes glare at the ceiling above as I resist the urge to let them roll in aggravation. My mother taught Michael and I various manners during my early years, which I've been careful not to let slip my mind.

The sighing under one's breath, the pouting of the lip, and the rolling of the eyes, simply because one is annoyed, is no reason to lose your poise; for they hold no honor and display the lack of self-command.

I smile faintly to myself. She was wise beyond anyone's years. Though her words are with me wherever I go, I do often have my uncontrolled moments and wish I was able to hold my tongue like she always did. She was the great encourager for Michael and me during any time of trouble. But I doubt Michael remembers her dark brown eyes or the gentle touch of her hand.

The front door squeaks, opened wide as Irene's bouncy figure rushes through on quick feet. "I heard you call, Mother!" She places a handful of lilies on the kitchen table, scattering bowls and spoons to make room for the flowers. "Sorry I didn't come sooner, I just got so enchanted by these lilies. Aren't they beautiful?"

I glance at the flowers and nod absently, grabbing a spoon to stir my tea.

"I need you to buy flour," Sarah directs her command to Irene, resuming wiping down each table and shelf with a rag, "Prepare the vegetables with Maddie first." She nods to the dresser above my head where utensils are kept.

Irene comes up to my side, retrieving two bowls. "Very wise of mother, as you could certainly use—um—*practice* in the kitchen." Her blonde head bobs up and down as a mocking stare glares into my face. I scowl, but accept the wooden bowl, hastening to the table board across the room. I grip the cup of tea with white-knuckled fists all the while, desperate to escape her remarks. She follows me to the table, holding out two ripe tomatoes until I finally set down the cup and reluctantly accept them. They'll be used for stew later on, a widely accepted meal in every colony.

"You must learn to cook like a housewife, mustn't you?" Irene prepares a bowl of vegetables herself, gathering carrots and onions to cut.

"From you?" I force the irritation in my veins to calm, sliding a knife off the table to slice. "It's not as if you do a finer amount of cooking than all the other young ladies in town."

She sucks in a sharp breath. "I do far more than you!"

I lean in, returning the challenge in her eyes. "Will you always think so highly of yourself?"

"Girls!" Sarah gives a light shout.

I shake my head, taking my anger out on the tomatoes, my tongue letting loose with a low whisper. "This isn't the 1600's anymore, Irene. We ladies can choose what to do with our lives." I peek over her shoulder, eyeing Sarah quickly then looking back to her defensive glare. "Some colonies are even allowing women to vote."

Her eyebrows shoot up, knife slipping from her fingers and toppling onto the table. "Living in the late 1700's does not make a difference when it comes to learning to make meals for a man!"

"Oh, please." My nose scrunches at her words. . . *make meals for a man.*

Uck! There is no earthly way that I, Maddie Holt, daughter of the courageous Colonel Holt, will be forced to make a meal for any man for his own pleasure any time soon! Glaring at Irene, I contemplate whether or not to throw another witty remark or one of the tomatoes at her vain self.

"*Think about that response going through your head before you let it come to your mouth, Maddie.*" The words of my mother float around in my mind. Her wisdom often keeps me from getting into mischievous trouble. I must admit, my words run wild when I'm not careful.

Still slicing tomatoes, I hear the pitter patter of a pair of muddy boots sound. "Michael!" I whisper, a smile spreading across my face. "Come here!"

I see the same smirk on Michael that always stays on Papa's lips, just barely there, but holding secret mischief behind each corner of the mouth. As he shuffles over from the doorway, I think again about how similar they look, yet Michael resembles a more playful version of Papa, his carrot colored hair matching his adventurous seven-year-old personality. My little brother looks up with curious, blue eyes, coming up to my shoulder, saying my name like its one of his treasures. My heart warms as he speaks through round cheeks.

"Yes, Maddie?"

I set the tomatoes down, wiping both hands with a rag. "Here." Reaching in my pocket, I pull out the chocolate stick. His eyes light with excitement as I grin. "And that's not all. I have another surprise for you." A twinkle gleans behind my eye as I run my fingers through his curly hair, the texture like Papa's. "It's in my—"

"What is this?" A voice rings out from the doorway to my bedroom. My eyes snap to the right, immediately spotting the piece of wood wrapped firmly in Sarah's palm. She holds it out in front of her with a rigid hand.

I step away from the table, pulse quickening. "Where did you . . ." I frown at the toy carved carefully to imitate that of a soldier in the American Army.

For Michael.

So help me, if I just left it carelessly to be found on the top of my bed.

How could I be so dumb!

"Where did *you* get it? I never sent you to fetch some useless toy." I cringe as she shoves the special possession in my face, its new and smooth wood glaring into my eyes.

I swipe her hand away, speaking through gritted teeth. "It is not useless. Uncle Henry made it for me because I asked him to. How is it any of your business anyways?"

Her nose scrunches, brow furrowing furiously. "It is every bit of my business as it is yours, young lady! Now you listen to me—"

"No!" I step backwards defiantly. "That is a special gift to remind Michael of Papa while he is away and you have no right to take it from my room. You're—" I falter, then raise my chin, speaking firmly. "You're not my mother."

She steps back up to me, fiery irritation in her mouth. "I *will* be."

A knot forms in my stomach as I stop, my voice barely a whisper. "What?"

"You're too young to understand, child." She huffs, triggering my confusion. Standing still, a chill works down my spine. Sarah's voice sounds ten times more booming than before. "Whatever were you doing at Henry's anyways? Is that where you've been going all these times I've sent you out to town!" I don't respond, my eyes falling to the ground, arms hugging my waist. "How did you ever find the money to . . ." Her voice lowers. "Maddie, did you—"

My head snaps up instantly as I push my confusion to the side. "Sarah!"

I study her eyes as tears fill mine at the brim. Such a feeling of betrayal fills my heart that I can't quite explain. My voice trembles slightly, dismay lying behind each word. "You actually believe I could be so dedicated to a piece of wood that I trade my dignity for it? You now assume I *stole*?" She opens her mouth as if about to respond, but I reach over and snatch the wooden gift from her hands before she can speak, slipping the toy into my dress pocket. "You see, the mother I was raised by actually taught me a little something about dignity."

I see her catch her breath as I glance at the tip of her nose and back to her eyes. I lean in, my voice lowering to a whisper as it wavers deep in my throat. "I *made* that money with my own hours. That's more than you'll ever do for this family."

She doesn't bother to pull on my sleeve or grab the loose threads of my dress as I pivot around, striding to the door. I turn the knob, stepping through, knowing I can only escape for a short time.

***

There's a certain thickness to the forest, seeming to crowd the trees closer together than they really are. The area is tight yet vast. It already comforts me as I watch its entrance and walk to the small pen behind our house, an excited neigh turning my walk into a jog. I soon stop in front of my beloved mare and step onto the fence in-between us. Her milky white mane is still the prettiest thing I've seen. I lean forward with affection. "Hey, Faithful girl." I stretch out a hand as she neighs in response, running gentle fingers along her face. "No time for riding tonight. Just going for a walk." Her head shakes with a loud snort, lips fumbling with my hair in discontent. "I know, I know. It's rough, isn't it?"

She's been mine for four years, a present from Papa when he learned I loved the giant creatures and had a desire to ride. If only I could take her through the great woods one more time and race freely underneath a green canvas, where I would marvel, above a white mane, at how it felt like the wind was carrying us. I press a palm to the bridge of her nose and warm the air with my whisper. "Just like we would with Papa and Patriot."

If only Sarah would permit it . . . but not so with Papa gone to war.

I try and ignore the way my throat tightens at the thought of riding with him again and step off the fence, planting a kiss to Faithful's nose. The forest beckons me, appearing dark and menacing yet being perfect for hiding. I run to it often, one of the tree's sturdy surfaces pressed against my back as I spend an hour thinking. Sarah only ever bothered to come after me once; luckily, I hastened to meet her closer to the house so she wouldn't discover my hiding place. She's never come after me since.

I dodge crevices and stumps along the uneven ground, a warm breeze sending the braid on my shoulder flying. Sighing, I wipe my brow with the side of my arm. My skin begins feeling moist, beads of sweat forming along my forehead and arms from the humid climate.

Loathsome summer is coming early this year . . .

Stopping, I stand by a particular tree, its trunk marked with signs of old age. Its lifeless branches hang low from the dry weather, sagging as if a burden weighs it down.

I circle around the giant plant as twigs crunch beneath my shoes, running my eyes over its rough surface indifferently and lowering to the ground. Doubts and questions plummet my thoughts. What I am to do next, where I am to go . . . if I'm ever to stay with Papa for longer than a week's time.

Too many doubts. Too many questions.

Knowing that I'm only digging myself an emotional hole, I shake my head firmly as if to get rid of the antagonizing thoughts. But they never seem to completely go away. Distracting myself, I continue gazing at the blue skies and wildlife above me. My ears tune into the hidden sounds of nature that take a little more attention to hear, including the sudden sound of a single twig snapping in half, bouncing off the nearby trees with a *crack!*

I gasp, lurching forward.

Faster than a blink, I dart to the other side of the tree so that I am concealed by its massive size. Sliding quick fingers into my boot, I grasp a blade and pull out, holding it at my side. I crouch low, grow still, and watch the open area lying ahead, waiting for the noise of another dead twig to snap.

Nothing.

Only the continual songs of various birds float in the air. I peer further around the tree as a breeze floats through. Brow dropping beads of sweat, I focus narrowed eyes, hearing stirring from behind.

My body tears from the tree, jerked by a hand.

3

STRANGER IN THE WOODS

I GASP UNDER THE pressure of fingernails digging into my skin. Two hands wrap around my arms, tightening, and twist me around in an instance. I grunt, pinned against the tree behind, locking eyes with . . .

. . . the face of a boy?

Instinctively, I place my palms flat on the chest of the stranger and push with all of my might. Kicking my leg out as he stumbles backwards, I hit him full force in the gut with my boot. He only loses balance for a moment, standing tall only two feet away.

I catch a breath, forcing a strand of hair out of my mouth. "Who are you?" I begin to circle him, putting distance between us with nimble steps. I run my eyes over him in two blinks.

His clothes say that he is a regular citizen, but his shoes are more sturdy, like they're ready to defend the ground on which he stands. A haversack wraps across his shoulder to his hip, several pieces of paper peeking through the top of the small bag. He shuffles to the side and back curiously, silent, seeming to relax once he perceives me as no threat.

I study the paper again. Parchment. The type that costs more than normal . . .

Messenger?

The stranger dips his head the slightest bit, peering under a mysterious gaze. My muscles tense more than before. His eyes land square on mine. "I was going to ask you the same question, Miss." The rasp in his voice is light. A mix of man and adolescent.

I stop in front of him, now yards away, clenching the blade wrapped by my fingers. "I asked first."

He stands with his hand on the bag, which I must assume holds a weapon of some sort inside. His brow furrows in and back up. "Do you really believe I would hurt a small, foreign girl like you?"

I quicken—"You're one to speak. You seem hardly of age yourself." It's obvious he isn't all boy. His height and strapping build add a look of valor to his demeanor, but I refuse to be impressed, tilting my head to the side. "How old are you anyways, twelve?" I flutter my eyelashes. "Perhaps thirteen?"

A winsome grin tugs at his lips, and he flicks a brow upwards. "You seem to have great intuition."

I return his narrowed gaze. It becomes clear by his stare that he has the upper hand, challenging eyes leveled on mine.

Just who does he think he is . . .

Suddenly the stranger turns casually, walking towards the tree I leaned against earlier. A short ponytail lies at the nape of his neck, dirty blonde hair held by a black ribbon. "I suggest you scurry back to where you came from if you wish to not tell me your name."

I stay in my place, feet planted on the ground. "If it is just a name you want, you could have asked for one before I insulted you."

A hint of mischief appears on his face as he crosses his ankles and lets the tree fully support his weight. "And are you apologizing for such a repulsive insult, Miss . . . ?"

"Hardly," I chuckle. "Though I would expect you to be able to stand such an offense if you really are more than just a—diminutive boy." I cock my head to the side, my mouth a sly smile.

He stands still for a short moment, then releases his grip on the flap and crosses his arms this time, his actions appearing more carefree by the second.

I wave my hand. "Are you not aware that I hold a dagger?"

"Oh—I am fully aware, but you won't use it. Yet, anyway."

I only furrow my brow at him with a beady stare, wanting to say something back, but not knowing what. He slightly grins at my hesitation, obviously pleased with himself. I draw in a sharp breath. "You're right, I won't . . . yet. But do not doubt my ability to slice with this thing. You wouldn't be the first I've used it on."

It's not a lie. Though only on animals for our dinner table, I have in fact used the blade. But, I'm sure I could cut through human skin just as easily enough to defend myself if there was ever a need. God forbid!

He adjusts a broad shoulder against the tree. "Tough choice of words for a child to use."

Irritated by his audacity, my brow furrows in. "I'm no child."

He remains silent. Eyes fluttering to mine, his hand slides into the haversack and makes me instinctively crouch.

I ready my blade.

But rather than a weapon emerging from inside, a ripe apple rests in his palm as he pulls his hand out.

He gestures to the fruit.

"Hungry?"

I let out a relieved breath, but continue to stay silent with knees still bent, ready for anything as I eye the apple suspiciously. Of course, it looks appealing, and it makes my mouth water. I haven't eaten in hours nor seen an apple so ripe and red in months. But I pull back and whisper in my head not to accept the delicious invitation, shaking my head stiffly.

"Don't say I didn't offer."

He shrugs at my reluctance, taking a wide bite near to the apple's core.

I ignore the tempting sounds of his chewing. "Might I ask again who you are? Or should I perhaps just pry the words out of you?" I glance at the blade, eyes then running down to his weaponless hand. "You don't seem to have much fight in you."

"Perhaps." He nods, but there's something else lying behind his eyes. "But really, Miss, you shouldn't judge someone that you've only just met so quickly."

"Ah ha, except we haven't met."

"So, you are willing to give me a name then?"

I shake my head like a parent aggravated by her persistent child. *And I thought I was stubborn.* "I also never said that I desired to meet."

"Well? Do you?" He smiles, prodding in a relentless way.

"Please. Stop with the child's play. I am simply a lady who has run into a suspicious stranger, and is trying to decide if he is only a local schoolboy!"

"Miss, I can assure you," his voice turns stern, "I am quite the contrary."

Noting how his words carry more grit, a light shudder runs across my skin. Then the playful tone that was there before comes back as if on cue as he lets out an impatient sigh.

"Though I can't blame a poor settlement girl for such bad judgment."

I tilt up my chin. "Must I remind you that you have no idea to whom you are speaking?"

"I can't help but hear pretentiousness in those words." He lowers the apple from his mouth and takes a few steps forward. I stay in my place but keep the knife at my hip ready for use. "But, you're right again. I don't. So, tell me then . . . why not end my misery and reveal who you really are?" His eyes glint mysteriously as his legs carry him closer to me. "What is it that you are hiding?"

"I might not be hiding anything. Pity for you really." My eyes flash, burning into his. "You'll never find out." Inching closer, he appears larger the nearer he gets. "However," hiding a gulp, I fumble backwards slightly, "I have just as much reason to question you as you do me, do I not?"

"True." With him standing now only a few feet away, I raise my blade higher as a threat. He raises his hands to show that he holds no weapon. "How about we introduce ourselves so that the suspicion will fade?"

I pause, making confidence sound in my voice. "I will always be suspicious of the people I meet until after long years of knowing them."

A lazy smile spreads across his lips. "Well, you have to at least start with knowing them." He glances at my only weapon. "Like civilized people . . ." His smirk stays in the corners of his mouth and it makes me doubt if I can trust him.

No, of course I cannot! It would be foolish to let my guard down, Papa would not be proud. Though . . . it wouldn't hurt to learn the young man's name.

Carefully, I lower the blade slightly and let it rest by my waist, still available for use. "Are you a messenger?"

He finally lowers his arms and stands still. "Ah— very observant. Yes and no. I do participate in the work of a messenger, but this time is . . . different," he trails off.

My curiosity beats any control of my tongue. "This time?"

His eyebrows shoot up. "It'd be my pleasure to stay a little longer and perhaps indulge you with stories of the dangers a messenger like myself encounters, stories so captivating they would make you swoon, but unfortunately, I'm needed elsewhere."

My mouth parts in a stumble to find a response, head shaking roughly. "I—"

He smiles playfully once again, like he's holding a secret wrapped up tightly in a covering, not willing to risk letting it be discovered, but tempting me to take a peek under it's veil.

My cheeks redden. I squirm uncomfortably under his stare, eager for his leaving. "Do you always smile so *cunningly*?"

His grin widens in satisfaction, charm etched across his face. "In all honesty, Miss, it's not hard to smile when there is something right in front of you to smile about."

My skin grows an even deeper shade of red, as red as the apple still in his hand. I glance at the ground in embarrassment. I've never been talked to in such a way by the opposite gender. I do wish someone would tell me, are they always this stupid with their words?

We stand there for a short moment, completely silent. I feel him studying me in an intriguing sort of way. He seems . . . eager. So very eager to get me to talk, while trying to act like he doesn't really care.

Perhaps he's just curious . . . who wouldn't be after running into a stranger in the mysterious woods?

I try to ignore the redness I can practically feel racing up my neck, asking the same question as before. "Where did you come from?"

He points a rough looking finger at me, the skin coated in dried dirt, it's cuticles peeling from lack of care. "Where did *you* come from?"

I shake my head. "This bantering is a waste of my time."

"If that were the case, you wouldn't still be here." He tilts his chin up with a sparkle in his eye.

"Because you know me so well now, do you?"

He flashes a smile. "I could! Come on then, where are you from?"

I contort every possible feature in my face. "Do you realize that your argument is completely illogical? You demand for my name when you refuse to give me your own!"

"As do you!" His face contorts back.

I huff, crunching the sides of my dress with both hands. "Just—how about we go our separate ways, resuming our own business? You said you're needed elsewhere, after all," I lightly mock, flicking up a brow.

He pauses and I watch him run a hand through his blonde hair. Ready to end this frustrating encounter, I pause as he suddenly walks closer, his steps cautious.

"Listen . . . I apologize if I've upset you." He lifts his hand up, pointing behind my back. "I shouldn't even be here. I'm supposed to be there."

My muscles tense instinctively. "River Springs?" I raise a brow and lower my voice. "What business do you have there?"

He takes another step forward, eyes growing softer. "You see . . . I'm looking for someone. *That* is why I'm so relentless about names. They're often my number one tool, the last piece to the puzzle. If I have something I need to deliver—" grinning, he pats the paper poking out of the bag at his waist, taking yet another step forward, "then I need a name. Otherwise delivering is nearly impossible." His grin softly fades, replaced with a flash of regret. "My name isn't important, Miss. I'm just a messenger whom I'm sure you will find no worth in remembering after we depart." He takes one more step, nearly closing the gap between us, and I notice that it's not just charm hidden behind his eyes, but also a past. Grief. Pain. Endurance.

This messenger is different . . . very different from ones that I've met in Papa's militia.

As I inch barely closer, intrigued, his gaze falls on the rest of my face, studying me with this gentle nature I've only ever seen in Papa.

There's always a twinkle in Papa's eyes. Always some sort of gleam. For a moment, it's as if that same twinkle hides behind the young man's eyes. The one that makes me feel safe, as though I'm being held even though there are no arms wrapped around me. I catch this odd resemblance between the two, perplexed at how alike something feels about them. I know it's not their features or hair color, but their presence, their manner.

Yes, that's it.

It's somehow the same.

He furrows his brow in, sweeping a thoughtful gaze over my face, and his boot barely brushes mine as he takes a final step. "This chat has been nice, Miss. But

I must leave." My lips fumble, body frozen as he strides past me. "I have duties. I can't explain, I'm sorry."

I whip around in ire, glancing upward and catching a Red Cardinal fly above, looking back down to eye the stranger taking urgent strides. My fists clench and my mouth curls. "You're just going to leave, just like that?"

"Maybe I should have been more clear." He spins, great annoyance shining in his eyes as they lie on mine. "If you wish to not give me a name, then I will be going."

He adjusts the bag at his waist, swinging it to his other side. He blinks once, twice, before shrugging his shoulders indifferently. "Fine. Good day, Miss." He nods, turning and proceeding towards my town.

My eyes linger on his figure, lips pursed. "Oh, for the love of . . ." A mumble slides out of my gritted teeth. "It's Maddie! Maddie Holt!"

He whips around in a beat. His eyes light with a sudden unbelief. Trampling thought leaves and twigs, an air of excitement takes over his steps. "Maddie Holt, you're Maddie Holt?"

My gaze stays on the excitement in his eyes and the vigor burning inside of them. "Yes . . ."

"The real Maddie Holt?"

"Yes, yes. I am." I shake my head in puzzlement, following his every movement.

He reaches down, searching through the bag I sense never leaves his reach. "What is it? Am I . . ." I trail off, my eyes casting down to the ground. Is Papa harmed? Captured? Worse? I look up with a snap of my head. "Are you here for *me*?"

He leans in, an impish smile on his lips. "I guess it's my turn to give a name." Though authority and decorum lies behind his voice, as does this hint of effortlessness, like the words roll off his tongue without much thought as he speaks. "Miss Holt, my name is Liam O'Dally, a messenger and patriot sent by Col. John Holt to deliver you a letter regarding our opposition." His voice lowers. "From your father."

I open my mouth, only to close it after no words come to mind. For a moment, I only stare into the eyes of a messenger sent on the colonel's behalf and can see nothing else.

"Miss Holt?"

Then I see the piece of parchment paper, perfectly folded, lying in his hand, waiting for me to retrieve. I see it's yellow hue, glistening faintly under the sun's warm bath. The mysterious messenger, Liam, nudges the letter closer to me, his smile fading.

Our eyes meet. My pulse quickens.

I wrap my fingers around the scratchy piece of paper, somehow sensing, feeling, hearing, already seeing the words of my Papa written inside.

4
THE LETTER

"MY DEAREST MADDIE,

Do not be anxious by this letter. I am writing to you because I know you are able to handle this information with composure.

We have reliable intelligence that the British plan to attack nearby in Salisbury. If they succeed, I believe they will try to march for River Springs next, though I cannot be certain. If they do continue to march, however, they will find you, because of your last name.

Be quick to get your brother and the girls out of town. Listen to my messenger, Liam. He will lead you all to safety.

I trust him with your life.

Be strong and of good courage. —Papa"

I lift my eyes from the letter, watching Liam. He curiously studies the branches above that form to make various shapes, hands slipped inside his trouser pockets.

I glance back down, hastily rereading a few of the lines written in ink.

'We have reliable intelligence . . .'

My fingers run over the paper thoughtfully as I bite my lip, smiling to myself. *Of course . . . that's why Papa's been gone for so long. He was gathering vital information on the British that must have just taken longer to get his hands on!*

"An intelligence advantage in the war," I whisper out loud, softly. "Perfect."

It will do us good, regardless of who draws in those despicable redcoats. I lick my dry lips.

"Liam, does this mean my Papa . . . he's fine? He's safe?"

He shoots me a glance, eyebrows drawn together disapprovingly. Dirty blonde hair sticks to the sides of his face in the pressing heat. "Miss Holt, your father is in the Continental Army. The promise of safety vanished the moment he volunteered to fight in this glorious war." He looks away, fumbling with his things as if suddenly in a hurry to complete this mission.

I frown, my eyes drawn back to the piece of paper. *I've always known Papa has never been safe. I haven't been holding on to some false hope . . . have I?*

This feeling of uncertainty lurks, looms even, uncomfortably in my insides. It taunts, whispering doubts that have never seemed to leave.

I open my mouth, then pause, steadying my voice. "He's—alive though?"

Liam's gaze raises, head still lowered so that the glare comes off a bit winsomely. "Do you always ask so many questions, Miss Holt?"

I almost scowl, but then notice the slight smile at the corners of his mouth, tilting my head and smiling back. "Only when the person receiving them is more stubborn than a mule."

"Harsh." He grins. "Alright, this mule complies." Winking, his arms cross, and his face turns suddenly pensive. "I received that letter three days ago. Something . . . could have happened by now. I can't guarantee anything." He looks downwards. "I'm sorry."

"Right," I nod slowly, trailing off, "I understand."

Don't fool yourself. You knew the chances of knowing anything for certain were low.

I've always known. Somewhere, in the back of my mind, where the thoughts of what could be true, what actually might *be,* silently linger.

"How long do we have, then?" I snap my head up, looking at Liam expectantly.

He sets the pack on the ground, walking a few feet closer. His steps suddenly seem more sluggish. He bites his lip for a long moment, obviously in thought. "Two days, maybe less," he finally says, his voice sounding drained of the life that was there earlier. Papa's never really mentioned messengers before. Not even of dangers they may face during their endeavors. But, Liam . . . his journey must have been quite difficult from the look on his face. So tired and worn.

He catches me eyeing him, raising an eyebrow as if to ask, *"Yes?"* I glance away, deciding to skim over the letter again.

Papa said he can't be certain that the British will be attacking River Springs next. It seems we have time to evacuate the town if they do attack. Besides, we have a handful of militiamen in town, prepared and ready to fight the Brits. Though so few in number, they would at best hold off the British long enough for some of us to escape.

Yet, something doesn't seem right.

River Springs? Out of all of the places they could attack?

"Liam?"

I look up at his expression, which seems to be growing impatient. "Why do you think the redcoats would spend their time attacking such a little town as Salisbury, or possibly River Springs? There has been almost no fighting in this area. Why now? It's not as if there's much for them here anyways."

He shrugs. "There's always something. Perhaps they're just desperate." He lifts his hand to the side of his face, scratching under his jaw. "But—I've thought about it too. It does raise some questions."

I nod slowly, then stand straighter. "Though I won't doubt Papa. I know whatever his reasons are, I can trust in them."

Liam turns to me, sincerity in his voice. "I've learned more from him than I can tell you. He's a good man, such an excellent leader."

"Yes . . . he is." I smile faintly, thinking of the comforting arms of my Papa that I haven't been able to run into for so long, my gaze traveling down to the ground. I used to feel secure. Protected. And now?

He's gone. Again. Far from home.

I glance away from Liam's gaze, peering past the trees and towards town.

Sarah will be looking for me.

I clear my throat, crinkling the letter in my hands. "Are we ready?"

He glances behind his back, towards town. "I suppose you should be on your way."

I pause, curious.

"Aren't you coming?"

Turning, he gestures to the trees, his voice sure. "I still need to scout the surrounding area." I raise an eyebrow, expecting more of an explanation, but he only offers a smile. I look down, refusing a blush as a bit of guilt rises inside of me.

"You don't trust me."

He reaches down for the pack resting by his feet, retrieving a wooden drum canteen from inside. He drinks, then extends an arm, offering the canteen.

I inch forward, furrowing my brow. "I guess as long as I trust what this letter says about the Brits planning to hurt the people I love, I have no choice but to trust you as well." Accepting the canteen, I allow cool water to soothe my dry throat, wiping my mouth once lowering the flask. "I must believe Papa when he says you'll get us to safety, don't I?"

Liam pauses, then nods hastily, seeming to agree. He takes the canteen, swinging his pack around his shoulder. "Right. Now, don't worry about conversing with the people about why you'll be leaving town, or even warning them of the possible attack for that matter—"

"Don't warn them?" My eyes narrow. I look around, disbelieving. "How could I not? They're my people."

He smiles. "We are only God's people."

I hold his stare, studying the look in his eyes. His voice firms as he speaks, but his eyes; they're soft.

How does he do that? Firm but sincere. Strong but gentle.

My chin tilts upwards. "Regardless, I still have a responsibility."

"Indeed." He raises his chin back at mine. "Getting *your* family out. That is the duty given to you by the colonel. Believe me, I understand that you care about the people in that town, but we are under the colonel's commands." Something flashes in his eyes. "We don't know who else we can trust."

I narrow my shoulders, confident. "You don't know them."

"No, I don't." His voice is suddenly firm. "But the colonel does, and these are his orders."

The confidence in him rises above mine as my eyes flutter. Some of the eagerness building inside of me subsides. His arms cross, tone softer this time. "They're not your responsibility. My men will make sure they are led away from the town."

I study him with a raised eyebrow, annoyed at his steady confidence.

He raises an eyebrow back, flashing a small smile as if amused, and my eyes almost roll. Never in all of my years have I met someone so vexatious yet likable at the same time. But more vexatious by a far, far amount.

I sigh, speaking forcefully. "My father is the colonel, and this is the town in which he resides. So, yes, I have a responsibility towards *these* people. By protecting these people, I accept my duty to our new country."

Both of his eyebrows raise this time as he pauses thoughtfully. "Just tell me then, how will you protect these people?" His arms stretch out as he speaks, motioning past the vast area of trees, as if challenging me to prove my point.

I pause. What would I do? I'm not as strong as a soldier, I don't have the skills of an officer. I'm not even sure who Maddie Holt is. Firm, or sincere? Strong, or gentle?

How can I be both?

Despite my doubts, I muster the courage to come up with a response, steadying my voice in an attempt to sound at least somewhat convincing. "I know how to shoot. I'm nimble, I can sneak in and out of town easily—"

"It's not enough." His voice interrupts, stopping mine. "You'll find yourself in the middle of a battle, surrounded by a large and malicious band of British troops." He takes a step closer, cocking his head. "Is that what you want?"

I pause, wondering if he sees a spark of excitement in my eyes, so I lower them to avoid his curiosity.

"If it's for the ones I love, yes."

Liam pauses himself, clearly surprised to hear such things from a girl. After a moment, he sighs. "Miss Holt, if I were to take a guess, I would say that your father loves you very much." His voice is light and easy. Effortless. "He needs you to be safe. Come with me. I'll take your family to my camp, away from the danger."

I note something different, a flicker of yearning that dances across his strong features, and it pricks my curiosity, but I only turn away. "I'm getting those people out." I begin walking past him, brushing his shoulder. He reaches out, taking hold of my arm. I turn, expecting to meet angered eyes like Sarah's.

"Miss Holt." There is not a hint of anger. His eyes are bright and deeply honest. "I won't know that you're safe if you spend too much time in there. We don't want to cause a town panic when we don't even know if the Brits will arrive. What I need . . ."

He pauses, thinking a moment before speaking again. "What your father needs is to know his family is safe. There is plenty of time for me to return and warn the town after getting you to my camp."

I hesitate, wanting to respond back. But I find myself standing still in his grip, stupefied, as I suddenly notice the color of his eyes for the first time. Rich and warm, two green pools stare back at me, like flickering flames and blades of grass all at once. My head snaps to the side and I harden, nodding curtly. "Fine. But only because it's what Papa wants, and only if you promise your men will warn the town in time." I twist, escaping his grasp.

He smiles, and this time my eyes roll. "I know. Papa's orders should have been a good enough reason in the first place." I turn, my back facing him. "I'm sorry. I tend to be a little more audacious than I probably should be."

I hear him chuckle. "You know, I believe that. Not that it matters now. We know our orders, and nothing should get in the way of them."

I nod, pretending to play along. Immediately, a plan forms in the back of my mind, and I make my decision. Liam shuffles around behind me, moving something in his pack. I have him where I want, he thinks I'll only get Michael and the girls, then head back.

But unknown to him, I'll send Michael, Sarah, and Irene to the woods, telling them where to hide until Liam arrives. And then . . . I will stay.

I can get them out. I can help them.

"Ready?"

My head snaps up, turning to regard Liam and nod firmly. "Where do I meet you?"

"Here. Same spot." He closes the flap to his pack. "I'll be back around dusk. Make sure to pack light, I won't be coming back with extra men to carry your things."

I nod again and he smiles, pulling his pack close to his side. "See you at dusk." He turns sharply and darts off into the darkening forest without saying another word.

I watch him go. He runs briskly, dodging trees and stumps, his figure slowly blending in with the darkness ahead where the forest grows thicker.

Dusk. I have a few hours.

I stand in the humid air, remembering the sincere look in his eye. It was an odd one, for only knowing me for less than an hour. He seems genuine. That should count as a good sign that none of this is just a scheme.

Right?

I frown in the dim light under the tree's branches, the thought suddenly occurring to me. What if he doesn't come back as the person he says he is? What if I'm only sending Michael into a trap, one he can't avoid once Liam—if that's even his real name—comes back with men intent on making them their new captives?

I feel a chill run down my back.

But I know that's Papa's handwriting . . . Is that enough?

It has to be. There could be men marching for my home, intending to hurt the people I love . . .

Annie, Lydia, Uncle Henry . . .

I sigh, still unsure of the circumstances, but deciding to trust anyways. My fingers run over something scratchy in my hand as I glance down. The letter still sits in my palm, crinkled around it's edges. I attempt to smooth out the crinkles, realizing I must have squeezed it too hard when talking with Liam.

Feeling another chill, I look up, peering through the jumble of trees. Why did he run? Doesn't he have till dusk? Perhaps that's just what messengers are used to doing. Running until they can run no more, breathing so hard until their throats turn dry, allowing adrenaline to build up until their hearts are pounding out of their chests.

I press my lips together, wondering what it would be like to travel the regions of North Carolina, perhaps even other states, rather than just one forest behind my home. I imagine the icy wind of winter in my face, trudging through a thick blanket of snow.

To just . . . be free. But full of purpose, always on a mission.

I shake my head, focusing back on the letter as something tears me apart inside. What's stopping me? Why do I hesitate?

Because that embrace he gave you three months and fourteen days ago, the one that made you feel safe, secure, at peace . . . might be the last he ever gives you. If you go.

I hear my mother's wise voice, her tone low, whisper soft and sweet. I know it's just my own mind creating the words, yet it's true. If I go, I might not make it out. But haven't I known all along that each day before Papa left for his three-month long journey might have been our last together? Couldn't that have been the last of many things? Our last hug? Our last shared smile?

Any day could be my last. I can't stay still, can't stay hiding, not while the people I love are endangered.

I exhale assuredly, starting to fold the letter back up. Then I stop short, one of the lines catching my eye, this time looking more distinct.

'... *they will find you* ...'

I shudder slightly, breathing in humid air.

Perhaps this is foolish. But they're my people. I know of this place as home because they make it home.

No, I can't leave them. I won't. I refuse.

5

Intruder Outside

MY HOME AHEAD SHOUTS *simplicity*, sitting in an open field, dark frame made of timber enhanced against light colored grass. The only reason Papa chose to build the house so close to town was because of his local duties to River Springs, ones he wouldn't be able to fulfill if far away . . . as he is now.

    I exit the forest dressed in sweat, hair sticking to my clammy and moist skin in a tangled mess. The sun's heat beats down on my skin without the concealment of the trees. The house is maybe a hundred yards away, so I pick up my pace. Dusk still won't come for several hours, but we'll need every minute to decide which necessities to bring and get back to meet Liam. I run through my head the most important things to bring with me, most important being my journal.

I smile, feeling the bulge in my dress's lower left pocket, where it always stays, hidden and safe. The small booklet is not the same as my other belongings. It carries the words of my mother that I never want to forget, every page filled with black ink, memories of her guidance and counseling written down.

Other necessities include a change of clothes, the canteen Papa gave me, the pocket Bible given to me by Uncle Henry, and a ribbon to keep my hair back.

I remind myself not to worry too much; most likely we won't be gone for more than a week. Our soldiers will guard the town, and we'll come back after they've cleared any threats.

Perhaps I'll even get to see Papa at this camp Liam speaks of.

I stop short, body freezing in between the house and the forest.

My eyes fall on a dark-headed figure ahead, a man sitting on a barrel at the back of our house. His silhouetted frame is just barely visible from where I stand. I frown, stepping closer toward the long-legged stranger, his clothing black as night and much more elaborate than what you can get in River Springs. Then

I hear a familiar giggle. A poised and thinner frame sits on the man's lap, feet swinging back and forth above the ground in mischievous delight. My pace picks up, eyes squinting in the sun to see her dress catch the light breeze in the air and drape freely over the man's knees. Then I see the way her hair glistens, golden locks reflecting the sun's light.

Irene.

Pushing my previous thoughts aside, I pick up my pace, now determined to find out why Irene, just barely sixteen, would *ever* be sitting on a such a stranger's lap.

The brat's been sneaking around with a—a man!

I practically gag into my hand at the thought, almost running now.

The dark-headed figure turns, easily noticing me approaching with the sun shining down onto my narrow form. He frowns, pulling Irene closer.

Questions plummet my thoughts. What is she thinking? Who is this man? The tall and dark stranger has to be a good four years older than Irene.

I'm still a few yards away, so I raise my voice to be heard, eyes locking with the man.

"Excuse me. You are on my property."

Quicker than a beat, I catch Irene's disdainful glare.

"*Your* property?" The stranger turns, speaking into Irene's ear. "Irene, who is this?" Irene holds my gaze, her face contorting as my eyebrows raise in question.

"No one, Warren. She'll be leaving." She squints at me, scowling under her tight lips. Warren looks back to me expectantly but doesn't argue with Irene.

I smile, turning to the stranger. "I apologize for being obtrusive during your secret gathering," I catch Irene's flushing cheeks, "but I must ask that you leave."

Warren pauses, then points to his chest, laughing amusingly. "Me? Are you serious? And just what are you going to do if I don't leave?" He frowns, pausing again. "Who are you anyways?"

He's anything *but* intimidating, though I can see he tries hard to be otherwise.

In one wide stride, I'm at the barrel. "I don't have to tell you that." His eyes squint incredulously as mine narrow, the tone in my voice steady. "Do not confuse me with a fool; no one in their right mind allows a stranger to continue lounging near their home." I glance at the wood behind his back. "Or a few feet from it." I lean in closer, and my eyebrows raise. "Off the barrel..."

"Oh, Maddie!" Irene's voice peaks to a pitiful wail, arms thrusting around Warren's neck with the exasperated fling of her wrists. "You may demand no such thing! Warren's my guest and he's staying! Isn't that right, dear?"

Warren looks away, acknowledging Irene. "Uh, of course, dear. As if I'm hurting anything anyways! Seems to me you ladies could use a man around this house." He shrugs, glancing back at me with a defensive wrinkle of his brow.

I suppress an annoyed laugh. "How do I know that you won't do harm? And Irene, this is my home, not yours. You are only here at the mercy of my father." I look at Warren with determination. "And he, the colonel, is already the man of this house."

He frowns, lips twitching. Irene's face reddens, but she has no time to respond.

"I'm sure you both are having the most marvelous time, really, but I insist, sir, that you leave immediately." I meet Irene's scornful stare and motion for her to follow. "Come on Irene. We have stew to finish."

She remains in his lap, clinging to his neck like a lost child. "Why would I *ever* listen to you?"

I cock my head. "Because I'll let Sarah know about this deplorable event if you don't. Why, she's sure to become enraged at the discovery of her own daughter sneaking around with a man nowhere near your age!"

Warren flushes deeply, releasing Irene. "I, uh, should leave you two alone." He slides off the barrel, forcing Irene to her feet.

I watch amusingly at Irene's baffled face. "Warren!" She makes two fists with her hands, hitting them against her sides.

"I'll see you later." He nods hastily to Irene and steps away from the porch. A look of annoyance intended for me shoots off his face, his tall frame passing by. I watch him go, his form growing smaller once he walks past the house and towards the main part of town.

"Well?"

I turn in response to Irene's demand, facing her crossed arms and mouth turned into a pout.

"Well what?" My voice turns into a half growl.

"Well, what was *that*?"

"Oh, please." I grab her arm, pulling her along with me.

She stands her ground, resisting my hold. "Let go of me! Ugh! Maddie!"

Halting and releasing her arm, I whip around. "Just what do you think you were doing, Irene? Bringing some stranger to our home? Has all sense left you!"

"I know him!" She rubs her arm exaggeratedly.

"Really? You know him so well from those few shared laughs and whispers on a barrel?"

Her chin quivers as her widened eyes suddenly fill with offended tears.

I resist a perturbed sigh, softening my voice. "Irene . . . if you want to get to know a young man, invite him to laugh and talk with *all* of us at dinner or something of the sort. Not in secret with no accountability."

Her watery eyes roll as she scoffs.

"Laugh and talk? I don't even think Warren could get you to laugh."

My weight shifts to one side, hands planting on the lower half of my hips. "What's that supposed to mean?"

She shrugs, folding both arms. "You know . . . lately you're just so stiff all the time."

Though I squint under my furrowed brow, I quickly dismiss her comment with a sigh, eager to end the argument. "Listen, Sarah will find out about—about *this*." I wave my hand, gesturing to the vacant barrel and hitting nothing but air as my eyes suddenly narrow in suspicious. "How long have you been meeting with him?"

She huffs under her breath, unresponsive. My lips purse, head shaking irritatingly. "Fine. But you can't keep meeting in secret like this anymore. It's just childish! Besides, why marry a guy if he's someone you would never introduce to your mother?"

"And tell me," she quickens, "how is this any different than *your* secret meetings with that little old man in town? The one that's been teaching you that useless drivel of a game? Oh, what do they call it? Ah, yes! Checkers?"

My teeth grit. "It's chess."

"So? It's still drivel, and he's still just a useless old man who will probably be—"

"Stop!" I cringe as my eyes flutter shut. "Do not speak of Uncle Henry that way."

She lets out a heavy laugh. "Well, why ever not? I am only speaking the truth—"

"You know nothing of the truth, Irene." I open my eyes and force a sharp breath through my nose. "My situation is different."

"How so?"

"Because it is," I snap, frustration boiling, pulling at her arm again. "Come on, we don't have time for this. I have an urgent message from Papa."

***

"You are a fool, child! Do you even know how dangerous those woods can be? There are creatures! Dangerous creatures! And other hazards! What if someone kidnapped you for heaven's sake?!" Sarah paces, shaking her head furiously. "I haven't any idea what I'm to do with you! What if—what if you ran into someone you knew nothing about, someone you didn't know was a threat or not?"

I raise an eyebrow, a mysterious messenger with piercing green eyes flashing in my mind, but do not mention the strange encounter. "You're trying too hard, Sarah," I sigh, leaning against the kitchen table with one hand. "You don't have to pretend to care. Really, it's alright."

She still paces, immune to my comments. "I just don't understand. I've done everything for you." I frown, letting her ramble. She suddenly whips around, facing me sternly. "What is it, huh? What did I do?"

My eyes narrow, studying her. I pause, reading into her intense expression, her eyes squinted, brow furrowed and top lip turned up disgustedly. I dare say she seems genuinely confused. But, there's more, there's something else. Anger, perhaps . . . anger at what? I open my mouth, hesitating, deciding to get to the urgent topic of Papa's letter. I try again, just like I did when first coming through the door to see Sarah's baffled face before she went off on her verbal rampage as Irene slipped into the back room.

I start, "Sarah, I came back to—"

"It's that Henry, he's been teaching you these reckless ways!"

Oh, for the love of . . . "I have a letter from Papa!" I shout, stepping forward. She freezes, stopping midway in between the kitchen table and the front door with eyes wide.

"What?"

I grip the letter, the sound of its paper crinkling in my fingers. "I have it here, in my hand."

She turns stiff. Her eyes go hard. A laugh projects from her wide-opened mouth. "Oh, child! He would have written *me*." Her hand flings in the air, but then she stiffens again, growing suddenly dark in movement as she inches closer. "Not *you*."

I wince and glance idly away, my voice a near whisper. "Just read it for yourself."

Sarah won't be happy with Papa's words. They were directed towards me, to make me feel stronger. I'm guessing they won't do the same for her. She grows still, eyeing the letter with a look of skepticism as I raise my hand, extending the piece of paper. Her face contorts and my eyebrows raise. She makes her decision, taking one giant step forward. Her fingers,

83

eerily bony and cold, barely graze across my own as she snatches the letter out of my grip. I huff, watching her fumble with the material she nervously forces open, her jaw set rigidly and lips drawn tight.

I move my hand to my forehead, rubbing the skin in vigorous circles. My eyes trail to the window ahead. Its curtain conceals most of the glass pane, pulled back only the slightest bit and revealing a stream of light from the orange sun outside. I stand straighter, ignoring Sarah's continued pacing, and walk towards the window with newfound curiosity.

How long do we have . . .

The curtain's rough material slides in between my fingers, scratchy against my skin as I pull back. Light immediately shoots through the transparent window, forcing my eyes to squint against the sun. The brilliant orange light settles low, resting just above the line of forest trees.

Maybe a little over an hour.

I smile, a sense of determination rising inside of me. It'll work. It has to.

"This is ludicrous. Completely absurd!"

My eyes snap away from the window, fixating on Sarah. I pull the curtain, stepping back to the table. "What do you mean?"

"You better explain to me why your father, my hus—" Her mouth clamps shut and my face goes slack. She fingers the letter in her hand with a hesitate tremble and speaks carefully. "I mean your father, him I mean, would ever put his daughter, of all people, in charge of this family." She grows hard again. "I'm the lady of this house!"

I squint at her, starting.

She hurries, "That's what your father hired me for, I'm here to run this household while he is gone and if this were truly from the colonel," she lifts the letter, "it would have been addressed to me."

I frown in bewilderment at her delusion, closing my eyes, shaking my head from side to side. "We don't have much time—"

"We have as much time as I say we have!"

My eyes open. "That's just foolish, even for you Sarah. Do you honestly believe I trust your judgment better than Papa's?"

She holds my glare and bites her lip, eyes holding such angst. She turns to stare at the wall ahead, arms crossed with the letter hanging close to her waist. "But this Liam person . . ." Her face grows eager, eyes perplexed as she whips quickly around. "Who is he really?"

I lift both shoulders in a shrug. "Who Papa says he is. A messenger. What does it matter to you?"

Her voice rises. "It confuses me why you would listen to a stranger! Don't you remember what I said about talking to—"

I harden, tired of her trying to replace my mother. "I have my reasons, Sarah. Papa trusts the messenger and so should we." She watches me as I push off the table and walk over. I reach out, lightly plucking the letter from her hand. "Pack as light as you can." I clench the paper, ready to turn on my heel and gather my things.

The boom of a cannon stops me in my tracks.

6

MEN IN GREEN

MY BODY LURCHES, JUMPING like a cat hit by water. Irene bolts from the back room, tattered dress swooshing above her ankles. "What was *that*?!"

No one answers, each jaw slowly dropping in a chilling mix of realization and fright.

Oh no. Please, God, no.

I act quickly, shuffling to the doorway in a state of confusion. My voice trembles over my shoulder. "M—Michael, stay here!" I reach the aging door, fumbling with its wooden handle. It swings open with one forceful pull, despite the shakes starting to run down my bare skin. I'm a hundred yards away from town, but I see it easily through squinted eyes.

The cannonball hits, it's paralyzing poundage ripping through the corner posts of a store as the roof caves in an instant. My legs move naturally, ignoring the voice in my mind that's saying something else.

This can't be happening. Why? How?

We were . . .

I quicken my pace, leaving the opened door and Michael behind. The dust and debris rising from the partially collapsed store draws me closer, beckoning my help and courage that's been waiting for a chance to act. The damage to the store more apparent, causing a deep moan to rise and settle deep in my throat. Another cannon booms.

We were supposed to have more time!

Suddenly I'm running as fast as I can, my body in motion on the familiar path. A crash sounds, and my head jerks to the closest corner of town as wood and iron collide.

NO!

My sprinting body stops short, breath catching with a sharp gasp. The side of Annie's shop becomes nothing but scraps of a fallen wall. I bear the sight of the entire side of the shop destroyed, the debris burying whatever life happened to be there under its heap of wreckage.

Miss Annie . . .

My jaw tightens, my eyes narrow, and I run. Distant screams echo off every shop, hollow and empty as my ears tune out and focus on the sound of my pulse.

Fast. Intense. Ready.

The center of town grows closer as the fiery burn from running starts in my abdomen and moves to my legs. I feel it's ache, and I let it feed my hungry desire to move. Annie's shop is just a few yards away, pulling me nearer to its once lovely interior design, variety of colorful treats, polished and fresh smell. But it's the thought of the body possibly buried underneath that forces my aching muscles to move like never before.

I approach the shop, dodging hunks of wood and debris. My throat dries out, an almost incomprehensible croak coming from my voice. "Miss Annie!" Whirling dust forces me to cough into my sleeve, lick my lips, and squint through the devastation. My boots trail through rubble, kicking up dust that layers my dress in a fine layer. "Miss—" I hack again, the cloud of dust engulfing the air. "Annie!"

My burning legs stop in the middle of the damage, eyes moving quickly. They sweep over the scattered remains of what was once beautiful wood. And my breath holds, as if it doesn't know how to do anything else.

So much destroyed. So much gone.

Miss Annie dedicated her life to this shop. Now what? Two more cannons sound, but I hardly even seem to notice. Is this how everything will be in the end? Damaged, fallen, broken?

Dear God, please. Help me find her!

A voice—so faint, just loud enough to be heard. It sounds again, to my left, muffled through the nearby screams.

I shout out, voice becoming stronger. "Miss Annie! Call out again!" A new strength appears, thoughts un-jumbling as my eyes anxiously run over piles of dispersed objects. "I'm coming, I'm coming." It comes back, this time more distinct. The voice is weakened, mumbling under the confinement of wood. I trudge through the clutter along the ground, spotting a—

Hand.

It moves, reaching through an opening in a pile of ruins stacked high.

I fumble through debris, making my way to the moving limb.

"Miss Annie!"

All the remaining strength I have gathers, surging through my arms as I lift pieces of shelves with a grunt. A large piece, taller than myself, conceals most of Miss Annie. She seems to push as I pull, the remains of the wooden countertop sliding to the ground with a loud *thud*.

"Miss Annie!" My eyes widen, knees bending down to scan for injury. "Are you alright?"

She sits up, seeming to grip the back of her head with a slight wince. "Yes, dear. I'm quite alright." Her voice is soft, not strong as it usually is. "Thank you."

I sigh a breath of relief. "Can you stand?"

She nods quickly. Her gaze changes, tired eyes turning to the scene behind me. "I don't understand." Her voice lowers, near to a whisper. "How could this be happening?"

I turn to the chaos in the street, my heartbeat louder than the screams. People run in fear, rounding shops and street corners though not sure where to go. Some shops have only minor damage, others are now reduced to what seems to be nothing but a pile of wreckage, littered across the ground where the business once stood. I sense the dreaded truth of what is happening. A surprise attack. What nobody was prepared for.

They were supposed to be in Salisbury!

There's something in the way the people are running, a queer sense of shock lying in every terrorized shout. They've never seen this before, never even heard of this kind of barbaric attack on citizens.

Because it was never supposed to happen!

And they have no way of knowing how to respond.

I turn, regarding Miss Annie with a new sense of urgency. "We need to go." My voice holds haste, and my eyes dart around with an air of desperation. The streets grow more awfully crowded by the second, buzzing with chaotic commotion and disorder. I silently thank God for the stories Papa told all those years. The ones I still dream about hearing. I realize now, in my spot on the ground, surrounded by the fallen beauty of the shop, that they prepared me for this very day.

I lick my dry lips, Miss Annie nodding along in agreement as I speak. "My house. It's far enough from town that we should be safe for awhile." I notice the loss of color in her face. "Are you sure you can stand?"

She's hesitant, but nods, rising from the rubble. "Yes."

BOOM!

We jump simultaneously. Our heads jerk upward, unable to see the iron agent of destruction we know is hurtling our way. My eyes shut, bracing for the crash, and I cringe as the sound of another shop falling echoes through our fractured, breaking town.

I steady myself, giving Miss Annie an anxious nudge. "Go. My house."

She stares at the full streets ahead, as if in a daze from the destruction of the cannonballs. I glance to the side, catching the remnants of another perished shop. These cannons . . .

They're so powerful!

I look through the circles of whirling dust again. My burning eyes land on a child. My throat tightens as I itch to run. Someone has to help.

Just get to one . . . save one.

I bound off the wood beneath my feet, barely feeling the hand behind me graze across my sleeve.

"Maddie! Wait!"

Her shout withers into nothing behind my back.

I leave with the assumption she will make it to the house, dashing off as fast as my throbbing legs will take me.

"Maddie!"

The sound of chaos grows along with the ringing of screams in my ears.

"It's *Michael*!"

I freeze, panting and briskly turning. Miss Annie stands further away with hands hanging loosely at her side, as if she started to run towards the house, but something stopped her, leaving her dead in her tracks. I follow her gaze, looking to the house. Then my heart drops to the pit of my stomach as I hope desperately that what's in front of me is not real.

Michael's short form stands in our doorway, flanked by two men dressed in a uniform I've never seen. Dark green vests and striking red jackets, swords ready at their sides. Black feathers bundled together at the top of dark helmets. It's something about the men, twisting my insides as I stand frozen to the ground.

These aren't normal soldiers. Papa told me—

I'm jerked backwards, the end of my flapping dress tugged from behind. I whip to the left, jumping sideways and falling into a pair of limbs, a hand sliding around my waist.

"I should have known to search the crowds for you when a battle calls," Liam does not smile, though his eyes are calm in the midst of the smoke and turmoil surrounding both our forms. His hand remains wrapped tight around my side. He pulls me further before I can process what is happening, dragging me backwards as his hand takes mine. We stop in between two buildings suddenly, hidden from the chaos.

He searches my eyes, fervent, voice raised above the cannons. "You need to leave with me! Immediately!"

My head shakes without even a second thought, only a fumble coming out as I try to say something that makes at least a little sense. "I—Liam, you—you were, I thought—"

"Thought I left you?" He shakes his head from side to side, sweat dotting his brow, and my thoughts finally clear. Quickly, I feel a panic rise in my chest, only able to remember Michael's small frame being led out by two strange men. A dreaded lump forms in my throat.

"Liam, it's Michael, it's Michael."

I slip my hand out of his, but he grips my wrist, pulling me to him.

"I know."

His grip tightens as a warning rises within me and thunders to even the blindest part of my conscious.

I *must* reach that wooden door.

"You have to let me go, please—just please let me go, Liam! Please!" Desperately shoving against his chest and the strength of his arms, a groan rises to my throat.

Michael.

Reach Michael.

"Let . . . go!"

"Miss Holt!"

His eyes snap to mine, a fiery stare keeping me in my place. His breathing quickens and his brow furrows. "You *can't*. If you go over there, they will only take you too. Don't you understand?"

"No," I squeeze my eyes shut and feel my hands shake, "no, I can't understand that!" I struggle to slide out of his hold, looking again to dart fearful eyes over his own. "Not when Michael's being taken at this moment! I won't leave, I won't!"

"Maddie, stop!" His voice cracks, barely heard above the sound of cannons booming. He grips my hands, bending down so we are level. Urgency and pain covers his eyes like a dark canopy. "They will take you, they'll—" He shakes his head, seeming just as broken as I as he bites his bottom lip. "I can't let that happen."

I inhale a shagged breath, looking away in frustration, feeling the weight of defeat. Though I push away from him still, a part of me relinquishes.

"I promise," he moves closer to speak into my ear in winded pants, the words being just barely enough to pull me along with him, "you will see him again."

He steps backwards, pivoting in the dirt as his hand grasps mine firmly. I stagger as I move, choking back sobs that I don't want to feel. We run, our shoes kicking up dust, and I don't dare look back, except for the moment that I do. I have to squint to see through the commotion I am hardly able to process, and past it all, I see him. Through the foggy lens of tears, I still see him.

A flicker of red, tousled hair. My own hair whips across my eyes as I barely make out my brother's small frame now forced onto a horse with one of the strange soldiers. They're quickly riding off with several other men in green vests as if they've accomplished their mission. I almost turn away, but I catch something else. Two other forms.

S—Sarah . . . Irene.

They lurk in the back, behind the house. I watch the two as Liam's hand still drags me along; Irene pausing by the house, careful not to be seen. Sarah hurrying nearby, backing further away from the house and seeming to beckon to her daughter. I still move, but my eyes dart between Michael and the people I'm not sure I will ever find the strength to forgive. Irene joins Sarah and they run, disappearing into the forest behind the house.

I turn from the image and silently wonder if any of this could really be real.

I'm sorry, Michael. I'm so sorry.

"Come on, through the trees." Liam's voice reaches my ears but fades just as quickly.

Stumbling into the woods, I realize Sarah and Irene are not the only ones leaving Michael. I do the same, and now I'm not sure I can forgive even myself. We move behind something rough, but I don't care to know what. My body is growing numb at the realization of what is happening. Bushes rustle, but I don't even fully hear it. The hand holding mine still pulls relentlessly, never stopping, still leading me further away to where light grows dim.

We only run. I have no idea for how long or how far. Then all of light is slowly gone, and I find myself growing still, hand slipping out of his, falling slowly, as if in a dream. The ground is suddenly a bed, tears that I didn't even know were there wetting the dry soil.

I'm so sorry, Michael.

My eyes shut like a prison door, a hole in my heart consumed by the sounds of distant cannons.

7

"They'll kill him, Liam!"

MORE THAN JUST THE dark looms.

I'm still held bound to the earth's floor by the same feeling that drew me there in the first place. A terrible feeling, a hopeless realization that there's nothing I can do except stay where I am. Away from somewhere I long to be.

The ground is soft, comforting, like how it felt in my mother's arms. I've never found the smell of soil pleasant, but now, as it wafts around my nose, the corners of my mouth draw into an unusual smile.

What happened before the ground beckoned me? Did I faint? Did I just give up and lay down? I reach back to remember, but all I see is myself falling into my own puddle of tears, slipping out of someone's strong grip.

My senses slowly tune in, the sounds and smells of the forest becoming apparent. A mesmerizing sound of branches swooshes above, singing a lullaby in harmony with late night critters, and the scent of crisp leaves is refreshing.

I fully realize where I am, yet I can't seem to understand *why* I'm in the company of the hovering forest trees.

Michael . . .

My eyes open at the thought of his name. I shoot upward, ears perking at the sound of leaves scattering under my arms. "Michael?"

Light, but rich, a welcoming voice comes from nearby. "Not quite." My beating heart grows more rapid as a hand slips into mine, rough fingers grazing against my own.

"Liam, oh." I fully rise, noting his looming figure barely visible by the evening's cold light. "Why are we here?"

His hand pulls, lifting me up from the consolation of the ground.

"More questions?" He grows more visible as my vision adjusts to the gloomy forest. His hands slip behind his back in a casual manner as his eyes catch mine. "Very well, then. We're here because you decided to plop right down without a warning during our adventure. I'm not even sure you consciously knew you had fell. I carried you as far as I could, then set you down before my arms fell off." I catch his grin and the furrowing of his brows under the dim light as I stifle a smile. He steps forward, his voice now serious yet calm as it lowers. "We're far out enough to be away from danger for awhile. I thought giving you time to rest would be alright."

Oddly enough, I feel myself grow warm in the face at the candor in his voice as a part of me starts warming slowly inside. I stare at the green eyes peering into mine and my head cocks, suddenly remembering what he said. "Danger? You mean . . ."

The attack.

I regard Liam with slight bewilderment. A breeze lightly soars through the branches, sending my braid's loose strands flying across my forehead and cheeks.

His words draw out slowly. "We need to leave for camp before they search out the area beyond town." His head turns around, scanning the area around us. I remember him doing the same as he rescued me from town.

My clouded thoughts clear, familiar senses of panic and fright coming back to me. My ears begin to ring with the memory of the sound of hoarse cries. The image of Michael's arms held back to two cruel men's sides stays burned in my memory, becoming bigger and scarier with every blink of my widened eyes. "But M— Michael. Liam, we have to get him."

"We will. When the time is right. Michael will be fine—"

"Fine? *Fine*?" I grip my dress, stepping forwards. He winces as my tone spikes. I feel myself growing angrier with every stream of words I let out. "We don't even know who they are. They fired cannons upon an innocent town. I can't imagine what will happen to Michael if they discover he's the colonel's son. I might as well plan his funeral today! They'll kill him, Liam! They'll *kill him*!"

"Miss Holt!" Pain flashes in his hard stare. His eyes lock on mine sharply. "They won't kill him. He's a child. They aren't *that* barbaric. They know who he is and they're using him."

I feel the tears forming in the corners of my eye. A sniff comes from my nose, and I squint hard. "What do you mean?"

He nods. "It's what they do. They'll keep him as bait, to lure your father in, or a good band of our troops they want dead."

I shiver at the thought of my little brother held captive, kept in a place of darkness or chains. A lump forms in my throat, making it a struggle to form the right words. "I don't, I don't understand. How am I supposed to get him back?"

"*You* don't." As he steps up to me, he stands at least a full head taller. "Your father will figure that out."

I almost oppose, starting, "But . . ." Frozen for a moment by the unwavering resolve is in his eyes, I realize that nothing is going to change his mind. I swallow hard, glancing downwards. An urge pushes me to glance back up, but the tears creeping over my cheeks keep my head down. I turn to face the other end of the forest and look up, a shaky puff of air coming from under my breath.

The woods have always been my safe haven, a place to hide where there are no eyes noting my every move, or irritated demands from the coldhearted woman trying to take my mother's place. Yet, the eery darkness to the thick mass of wooden plants sends a shiver down my spine. I want to run back, to somehow rid my town of any threats. But a lingering part of me also wants to leave all of it behind. To only search out Michael, to just run further into the clutter of the branches ahead, immersing myself in the smells and sounds of nature hidden beyond the forests of North Carolina.

A tinge of shame rises at the thought of wanting to leave home.

Papa wouldn't leave.

I sigh aloud, annoyed at my indecisiveness and racking my brain for answers to the countless questions arising in my head. "What's happening, Liam?" I ask it more to myself. "Papa's letter. It was all . . . wrong." My fingers run through the tangled mess in my hair. Whatever information Papa and his force had gathered, it wasn't accurate. Unless it was, and Salisbury is still a target for the Red Coats, but they decided to come to River Springs first.

As I turn back around, Liam studies a branch hanging just over his head, raising a hand to prick a leaf from a stem. "Information from spies is always sketchy. They were right that an attack was coming. Just off on the timing and the first town to be attacked." He glances to me, spinning the leaf. "I suppose there's nothing we can do about it for the moment." Then he releases the leaf, swiping both hands across his shirt. "At least you're safe for now. We need to move."

I nod, tempted to look at the trees behind as the tint of guilt rises again. Liam adjusts the bag still around his waist. He turns, and I reach out to grab his arm with eyes wide. "Wait, Liam." He studies me with a peculiar gaze as I inhale a shaky breath. "I won't be able to bear my guilt if I leave them." My muscles are tense waiting for his response.

His voice is low, almost solemn as he responds. "You have to pick your battles, Miss Holt."

A twig snaps under my shoe as I shift to lean on my other leg. My whisper is almost spacious compared to his, lingering in the air after each breath escapes my mouth. "What if I don't know which one to pick?"

I can practically feel his whisper. "Then follow your heart."

It speaks to more than just my open ears. It's like my own language, singing to the deepest part of my soul. If only I knew what my heart was telling me. I long to help the people, my family, regardless if they have the same blood or not. More than just names, but faces and memories come to mind, an ache taking over my whole body.

Miss Annie and Lydia . . . Uncle Henry . . .

"But also heed counsel from those you trust." Liam's voice comes back. "Your heart and feelings can fool you, but there is wisdom in a multitude of counselors. I've watched both your father and General Washington follow the advice of those around them and it has served them well."

Liam sighs, edging closer. "I don't think you exactly understand what a dreadful state you will find that town in."

I quicken—"Which is exactly why I must go back to help."

"No, it is why you wouldn't be able to do anything. There would be too much disaster, too much tragedy.

It's more important that we get to your father and begin a plan to get Michael back."

I wince in the moonlight beginning to creep through the branches. I'm not able to bear the thought of the people being held captive or losing everything they ever loved. But I'm also not able to bear the thought of what will happen to Michael if we don't get him back. A moment passes as I watch the ground, and his voice comes back quieter this time, hardly confident.

"We'll get Michael back. I'll see to it. I promise you."

My head snaps up. "You can't promise anything. Did you see those men?" I walk closer to him, suddenly starting to boil inside. "What will you do? Is there even anything you *can* do?" My tongue gets ahead of me as I realize full well the unfairness in taking out my frustration on the very person that saved me. "If so, then do it! Send troops! Why can't you? Why—"

"It's not in my authority, Miss Holt!" His eyes widen, silencing all noise from me and the forest. "Do you not understand that I am only a messenger?" He looks around, lifting his shoulders and furrowing his brow distressingly, angrily. "I—I can only send a few scouts, not a band of troops!" I almost turn away, grimacing, when he lets his shoulders fall and breathes in and out heavily. "I'm afraid you put too much confidence in me." His forehead creases, something more sorrowful flashing in his eyes that I haven't seen before.

I hold my breath, feeling my lip give in to a quiver. My hands hang at my side, lifeless. "I guess so." I nod, void of hope. "You're right, you know." I ache, mad at him and mad at the One who could have stopped it all. "I'm sorry I ever put any ounce of trust in you. You're little more than a boy." He only stares, as if having no strength to respond. I blink wearily and find nothing else to say.

I know my words to Liam are completely unreasonable and regret already stings my conscious. But why didn't God stop any of this? Why isn't Michael safe? I want to fight. I want to run. I need my brother back. Sniffing back a despaired cry, I walk slowly up to him, chin tilting up. "I don't care what you do." I steady my voice under his deeply seething glare. "But I'll never forgive myself if we don't find him."

He pauses, and for a moment I think maybe it's sympathy lying in his eyes. "Maddie." It's the first time he's called me by name. He inches closer, almost cautiously, appearing to choose his words carefully. "I know you want your brother back. I know you want to do something, anything." He clenches his jaw, eyes dancing back and forth from both of mine. "But this is out of your hands." I breathe in, folding my arms against my chest. My head turns away frustratingly as he starts again.

"There is nothing we can do right now except get back to camp with a report and get to your father. The hardest part is realizing that these things take time. It may take weeks to get Michael back." I look up thoughtfully, reading his face that seems to settle into weariness from trying to convince me. He shakes his head firmly. "But they won't hurt him. They know that type of cruelty would backfire on the entire British Army. We have to keep our wits about us, take the next step in front of us. Trust that God will make a way for us to get to Michael."

I want to respond, but the fight has left me. Whatever little rest I got when Liam let me sleep has certainly not replenished what this fateful day has taken.

"We're not far from my squad's camp. Let's keep moving."

I nod reluctantly, beginning to follow in silence. Did he really say it could take weeks to get Michael back? Is this what it's like to be in the war . . . rather than just reading about it? This feeling of urgency and crisis, is it a constant for those in the battle? How does Papa stay so calm in the middle of chaos? Have I mistaken Liam's calm for not caring about Michael, when in fact he's learned from Papa how to act wisely while others are lost in distress?

Maybe this is what Papa meant when he always quoted that Scripture. What was it? Something about not having fear, but rather power, love, and a sound mind.

That's what I need right now.

I stare at my shoes, taking short strides, lifting up my heart.

Father . . . I don't understand why You would allow this. But I will cling to You. I will hold on to Your promises. Give me strength. If power, love, and a sound mind is going to help get Michael back, then please take away this spirit of fear. Please guide me. I feel lost. I don't know what to do or where to go.

Yet, You had Papa send this messenger to me just in time. So, for now at least, I will take this sign of direction and follow him. Wherever he goes . . .

I lift my head to the trees as Liam leads. My boots shuffle through dead leaves as I follow like a lost soldier waiting to arrive home.

8
Loss and Trust

FOUR MEN DRESSED WITH the faces of courageous soldiers gather around the repose of a fire. A musket accompanies each of their sides or leans against something nearby. Liam has already briefed them on the attack at River Springs. None of them are shocked, as if it is a daily affair.

Now he turns and gestures to me.

"Men, this is Maddie Holt. Miss Holt, your father's bravest and most valiant soldiers from this side of North Carolina." Humor drips from Liam's voice, though my shoulders still shudder with fear.

"Now, O'Dally, I believe you mean *all* of North Carolina. Pleased to meet you Miss Holt." The soldier nearest to me flashes a grin, one foot resting on a large rock, elbow on his bent knee and chin resting on a folded fist.

Liam's low chuckle resonates in the quiet night. "My mistake." He looks to me, then throws a nod at the soldier. "This is Woods."

I cock my head the soldier's way, rubbing my arm. "Woods? Is that your real name?"

He reveals nearly straight teeth, the corners of his mouth curling up into his dark scruff. "Maybe."

I pause. Then the furrow of my brow disappears, and my lips give in to a fond smile before I can resist. Liam gestures to the man on my other side, who is unmistakably Indian. "That's Tomah." My eyes widen, previous thoughts of panic shoved to the side.

A real Indian?

His shoulders are broad and he's easily the tallest of the group. Red skinned and dark hair at the nape of his neck. Not only a musket stands at his side, but a long blade rests in a sheath attached to his hip, an animal hide wrapped around its handle. Undoubtedly a weapon of his people.

The Indian nods, something mysterious yet welcoming in his eyes catching mine.

"Dawson Kelly next to him." Liam looks at me and smiles. "We call him Kel." The third soldier is red headed with piercing blue eyes that flash in the firelight. "Ma'am," he says, as if it's a whole sentence.

"And this old man," Liam tilts his head up, relaxing into his easy posture, and I find the fourth man's eyes, "well, that's Jackson. Grandpa Fields."

I raise a brow. "Fields?"

"That'd be my last name, Miss. Honored to meet the daughter of the greatest colonel in the Continental Army." The man winks, voice rough like sand paper. Brows bushy and dark, his eyes crinkle with a hidden glean.

I glance from man to man, their scruffy faces illuminated by the dim glow of the burning fire. Of course I've seen soldiers in my lifetime. But there's something different about the way these men are so carefree, even in the midst of a war, as if everything comes naturally to them. They look about the tiny camp with a confidence in their eyes. It gives me a queer feeling, making me curious to know how they came to be so.

Liam is saying something again, but I hardly even notice anymore. The atmosphere of the small, makeshift camp demands my attention. There isn't much to it. Each man seems to have his own space around the fire, logs or large rocks upon which to sit, weapons and satchels close by. Everything seems to be organized in a compact way, ready to be packed in minutes. But for the moment, these unusual soldiers seem relaxed, even knowing how close danger might be.

Almost immediately, the stories come to life. Finally. I see a part of them with my own eyes. It's Papa's world, where he sleeps and spends every night, with the camaraderie of his fellow soldiers. I scan the men again, realizing something else. My eyes linger past the glare of the fire and I squint. Red and blue color the men's garments, white sashes across the front.

I snap my eyes up, excitement flicking both my brows towards the sky. "You are Continental soldiers?"

The men pause, all four sharing glances. They erupt in chuckles simultaneously. One of them rubs at the beard under his jaw. "Now, Missy, that would seem quite obvious, as we are wearing the required apparel, and have you noticed how gentlemanly we are?" The redhead, Dawson, nods my way and reveals a contagious grin. "Militia men aren't as gentlemanly."

I return the smile, looking to the others and turning to Liam. "Why didn't you tell me?"

His voice quiets, eyes holding mine with a spark inside them. "I figured you'd have known."

I look to each of the men quickly. "Most of my Papa's stories have come from his times with the militia. I guess I assumed, when Liam mentioned we'd be meeting with my father's men," I glance at Liam for emphasis, "that you'd all be with the militia." I look the men up and down, hiding a small smile, biting the corner of my lip. "I should have known."

The men smile in response to my innocent shrug. One of them, Woods, stands a little straighter and cocks his head. "Are you suggesting we would have been more commendable as militia men, Miss Holt?"

A quick breeze sends my arms around my waist as I stifle a short laugh. I tilt my chin to show him the resolve in my eyes. "Not at all."

My gaze wanders with my mind to the fire as the men converse. Talks of the war, other nearby camps, and how training for the Army is progressing. Their voices never raise much above a whisper as we all watch the misty smoke from the fire rise into the night sky. My questions resurface, refusing to be ignored, begging to be put to rest. I furrow my brow, the slight breeze clinging to my skin, more chilling as the night grows heavier. The details of the attack seem so vague that I don't know what to make of them.

The letter, rough in my hand. I can still feel its parchment and strong smell. Papa *had* said they were suspicious . . . they were so close. So close to finding out in time. I pause, my eyes narrowing at the ground, and more than the questions resurface. This time they're accompanied by a feeling, one suspicious and disturbing. It creeped into my mind during the attack, sending a tremble to my limbs. Black feathers, green vests. Men that I know, and yet don't. Does Liam know?

" . . . don't be shy, Miss. Just make yourself at home."

My head snaps away from the fire, realizing the statement was aimed at me. The men have begun laying down in their own spaces around the fire, using their satchels as pillows. I give Dawson a grateful nod before turning to Liam. "We're not moving tonight?"

He sighs, raising a hand to rub under his jaw.

"We'll be safe here. Tomorrow will be a long day, we won't reach the main camp until dusk, so tonight's sleep will be vital."

They begin making room for Liam and me to each have our own space around the fire. The older one, Fields, pulls a thin blanket from his bag and spreads it out for me. Woods offers his own small leather bag to me. "It's the closest thing to a pillow you'll have tonight."

I nod. A nervous swallow comes from deep in my throat as I decide, making my choice, forgetting the disagreement from earlier in the woods. I lean in a bit closer to Liam and force my breath to steady. "Could we talk?" I glance at the other men and lower my voice. "Please?"

He seems to pause in surprise, then rises and offers me a hand, helping me up.

We turn to walk, and my eyes wander as we approach a barren area still close enough to the firelight, but where I feel I can talk without the others overhearing.

I will myself to put the right words together.

Say something.

I attempt to open my lips.

They stay sealed, Liam looking to me expectantly, and the questions about the daunting British men disappearing at his lingering gaze. Heat rushes to my skin like a wild fire.

Say something!

My shifty eyes bounce to the ground and back up, my cheeks flushing even as I say the words. "Uh—this camp is cozy. The fire's pleasant."

His head tilts, and a small smile spreads at the corners of his lips. "Mhhm."

My hands fold behind the small of my back.

Mercy. A soldier. Amused at me.

I focus on the ground, ashamed at being so flustered. Why am I fumbling with my words? Never have I acted so . . . so . . . oh, so!

"You don't always have to be so tough." He snaps my attention from the ground. "You know that, right?"

I let out a whisper that comes out more like a rasp, the words I actually planned on saying slip forever away into oblivion. "Pardon?"

"You haven't seen your father in over three months," he remarks, gently.

"And?"

"I can imagine it's been hard, that's all."

I suddenly realize that I'm holding my breath. I let it out. "I—well—yes. It's hard." It aches a little to give a smile, but I do.

Already, the snores around the fire make their way to us and we both let out a light chuckle.

We grow silent, and another thought occurs to me. I shuffle, straining to see him more clearly in the moonlight, voice lowering.

"How did you know how long it's been since I've seen Papa?"

He pauses, seeming surprised by the question. "Your father, he and I talk."

"Talk?"

"Yes." He runs his hand through tawny yellow hair.

I press my lips together, flushing at the growing silence. Liam quickly gestures to the side, taking a step. I follow his lead, turning to head back for the comfort of the campfire, amazed the others are asleep so quickly.

"So, what do the two of you talk about?"

He walks with an easiness, carefree and light in his strides. "I don't want to bore you. You know, muskets and strategies and all."

My eyes grow big, stomach fluttering. "Oh, I would give anything to fire one of those muskets in an actual battle. I practice shooting every time Papa's home, but to have the grit to shoot and reload in the face of a real fight? It must be exhilarating."

"Really?" He turns, arms crossing as we approach our places by the fire.

"Really what?"

"You sound like you've actually thought of being a soldier?" He lowers to the ground with a furrowed brow, and shrugs. "I guess I thought girls had no interest of the sort."

I hesitate, finding my own place on the tattered blanket given by Grandpa Fields. "Well, maybe most girls—"

"And firing weapons," his voice deepens, as though he's analyzing something. "I mean, for a girl, isn't that not very . . . safe?"

I snap my eyes to meet his, jaw set tight. "Not if you know what you're doing."

For a girl?

He raises both eyebrows. "So, you do know how to handle a musket?"

I nod as he leans back, his palms landing on small patches of grass on the dry ground. "I'm sure you'd know what to do if one of those guns were in your possession. It's just, I've never heard of a girl with a thing for dirt and grime, let alone the horrors of war."

I raise a brow, teasing in an almost pathetic way, as if just trying to forget all that's happened in the past few hours. "Well, I never said dirt and grime. I wouldn't dare ruin my dress."

He looks my way. "You just get more prestigious by the minute, don't you Miss Holt?"

I look away, hiding a smile. As I glance back to him, I soften my tone. "I do wish you would just call me Maddie."

He flickers a glance to my chin, back to my eyes. "Okay. If you insist."

"I do."

I shift my attention to the stars, to the way they shine perfectly bright during these first nights of summer, and slide until my back is flat against the ground. The twinkling in the dark sky calms me at least a little, keeping my mind off what I can't control. I tilt my head to face Liam more, but my eyes stay ahead. "What are all of you? I mean—if not a militia?"

He clears his throat before responding and shifts closer. "We were—chosen—I think is the right word, by your father."

I furrow my brow. "Based on what?"

"On what he's looking for in a soldier for this unit. Gumption and expertise. Unique skills. Stuff like that."

I turn to him, playfulness in my tone. "And you have enough stuff like that?"

He glances at my eyes and smiles.

"Impressed?"

I shift my head on the satchel, a soft wind cooling my ankles stretched out below my dress. "You seem to greatly enjoy humoring me." I hide a grin and fold my hands against my stomach. "So then, what does that make your little band of skilled soldiers?"

He sighs aloud. "I'm not sure what you'd call it. We are just his men, ready to be wherever he needs us."

"Sounds a bit like minutemen to me," I suggest in thoughtful tone, raising my gaze to his.

He sits up slightly, leaning on his side and his elbow. "You could say that. Your father was looking for something different. He is different himself." Excitement fills his voice. "Like the great men. Generals Washington and Henry Knox. They believe this army doesn't just need soldiers, but patriots of the most spirited kind."

I nod. "And you agree?"

He pauses for a moment, then turns to lay back down, eyes lifting to the sky. I study his features intensely with a thirst to hear him speak more of my Papa. "I do. I believe we won't win this war without men like your father." He turns again to face me. "But because of what I've learned from your father, I believe we can do all things with God. Including winning this war."

Now it's my turn to turn away and gaze upward. "I always thought that too. Until tonight."

"And now you don't?" He seems to genuinely wonder.

"Well, no, I guess I still do. It's just, some things, they just," I feel his gaze but remain focused on the stars, "some things require more than just trust." My voice barely raises above a whisper. "And some things shake your trust."

The fire crackles as he waits a moment before responding. "Without trust, we won't make it through anything at all. Trust is what keeps us going, it gives us the ability to hope." A ring of kindness joins the words he seems to strongly believe, sounding so much like Papa. "Take away every comfort, every other ability or strength, but give me the faith to trust in God, and it will be all I'll ever need."

I start, pausing, and starting again. "You've been talking a lot with my father. That sounds exactly like him." I turn to him, frowning. "And I do still believe that. But the thought of Michael being taken away, the destruction I saw tonight, I, well—" I frown, deciding to be vulnerable. "I don't understand how God could let that happen."

"And that, Maddie, is where the trust comes in." He sounds understanding, like he's on the other side of the mountain I'm climbing. "It's easy to trust God when everything is going right. But when you see what I've seen in this war, well, let's just say some people stop trusting at all and others begin trusting all the more."

Slowly I peer at him, studying his features in deep thought.

"At first I was one that stopped trusting." He pauses, swallowing. "The more I lost to this war, the more I lost trust. But then I met your father." He locks eyes with mine. I raise a brow, smiling slightly. His confident tone draws me to hear and listen. "It's not just things he says, it's what he does, how he lives, how he responds to things that happen. His courage gave me courage. His faith built my faith. And his trust," Liam nods firmly, head against his blanket, "his steadfast trust built my trust in God as well. Even in situations where things just seemed to get worse." I keep his gaze for a moment, and he grows quiet. Lowering my eyes, I know he's only saying what's true. I know that I must trust. If not, what else can I do?

I steady my breathing and close my eyes.

God, I know what You say . . . that You know the plans You have for me, even though I don't. Plans for good and not for evil. With a future and a hope.

The verse sounds in my head . . . Jeremiah 29:11. My comfort verse in times of uncertainty, words from God Himself, full of assurance.

Help me to believe in it. Thank you for sending Liam to remind me of what Papa taught.

Of course, Papa also always pointed out that those words of comfort from God were given to the children of Israel as they were being marched off to seventy years of captivity!

Even through captivity, God's promise of good plans still stood.

Can I still believe those words with Michael being captured? Does God have plans for Michael that are good, and not for evil?

Silence grows, and my ears catch the sounds of crickets, the gentle breeze playing with branches, grass atop grass as the same breeze sends them swaying. I let my eyelids grow heavier.

Liam's whisper—"You're like him, your father."

My eyes snap open, shifting to him.

"You have his same spirit and determination. You're perhaps more stubborn, but nonetheless . . ." He casts a crafty glance my direction, triggering the furrow of my brow.

"I am *not* stubborn."

His smile widens, sweet as honey. "I knew the moment I ran into you that you were more stubborn than most."

I tighten my glare, stifling a laugh of my own and sighing. "I see some of him in you too, you know."

He shifts in his position on the grass. "A good thing, I'd say."

I nod in agreement. "I'd say so too."

"It's a true honor, really, for him to befriend and mentor such an ordinary messenger." His voice is low and clear combined with the hushed sounds of nightfall. "Your father is a very generous man."

Propping up on an elbow, I look back to see an almost guilty look in his eyes. "Liam. I know my father. If he chose you, I'd think you to be more than just an ordinary messenger." I want to say something more, so I give a slight smile. "But I think you're more than that anyways."

His eyes stay on mine, his whisper smaller than the breeze around us. "Thank you."

We settle back into silence, despite the questions running in my head, and I savor the stars. Hearing

Liam's breath in rhythm with mine, I'm grateful for the presence of someone Papa sent himself.

Does Michael have the security of another person by his side that he trusts and knows? I think about what he doesn't have, what he never will if I don't get back to him. Without a fire or blanket, he could be cold. Without the cricket's song, what if he is unable to find sleep? There's no me for him, no Papa, no comforting goodnight kiss.

An anger resurfaces, not understanding how he could have been taken away, why this was allowed.

How can good come out of this, God?

I finally glance back to Liam. "How do you think Papa didn't know . . . what was coming, I mean?" My eyes lower from the stars, falling to the bits of flames shooting off the dying fire.

"I'm sure your father did all that he could." His tone is gentle.

I force my breathing to steady, briskly wiping a finger under my eye to catch the tear. "You're right. It just doesn't make sense."

He eases up on his side, gaze locking with mine. More intense than before, pain flashes across his every feature. The blurring continues in my eyes before I can stop it.

Liam swallows, glancing down. "Maddie..."

I feel a lump form in my throat, keeping any words from making their way out. What is there to say?

"I'm sorry." His voice breaks with the last words. "I've said everything else but that, and I should have already said it. I guess I've just been caught up in getting you to safety and haven't told you that I know this is hard for you. That's just it, I know exactly..." He trails off, looking down and shaking his head as he stops mid-sentence.

How could he know exactly how I feel? Has he lost someone? I cringe at the thought.

"I'm just sorry this is happening to you."

"It never—" His breath catches, eyes narrowing. "It's tragic. I guess I've seen so much of it over the last few years that I forget the brutality of the British is something you had not seen up close until today."

He seems to wait, like he wants to say more. Then the lines in his face ease and he straightens.

"Let's get some sleep, tomorrow is going to be a long day."

"Liam, it's alright. I'm sorry too. I was completely out of line with the things I said earlier. About you not being able to do anything. You've already done so much. You saved me tonight. You did what Papa sent you to do and I'm thankful. I don't show it very well, but I am."

I hear him gulp, seeing him close his eyes as he turns to lie flat on his back. "I didn't do what your father wished. I was supposed to get all of you back to him and I failed."

My body turns cold as I think of Sarah and Irene escaping.

"But I'm going to make it right." His whisper is calm, determined.

I have no idea how to respond, so I say nothing. But the pain and the determination in his voice plays over in my mind. It's as if he wants to save me from an even greater pain than I feel now. A pain he clearly knows.

The pain of loss.

9

Four Dragoons

THE SMELL OF CRISP leaves and summer air meets my nose. It's a pleasant smell, reminding me of the days Papa would take me far into the woods, where it was thickest, to find wild game for dinner.

The soft padding of our boots sounds against the soft ground, and we creep among sleeping trees. Everything feels still, as if the wood beneath the leaves has stopped aging. The birds themselves seem to understand that danger still looms, now hushed in order to not be discovered.

I keep my eyes on the bobbing heads of the soldiers ahead, steps silent.

We had left at dawn, just when the day was at its coolest. The men took turns taking watch throughout the night, so I know they are more tired than they are willing to admit. I can tell by the way their steps are slower, how it's easier to keep up with Liam than the night before.

My eyes focus ahead, but my mind drifts to later, to what follows. Papa, Michael, home, family . . . what can I do?

Three months and fifteen days.

It won't be long before the separation between us is no more. I'll finally get to settle in Papa's embrace again, where there's no such thing as fear.

A small smile spreads across my lips.

We slide around a tree, only to dodge one after another, like navigating through a never-ending maze, and a click from Liam's tongue sounds behind me.

The men halt.

Spinning, I catch Liam's hard expression.

His brows draw together tight, and my head cocks in the same perplexed way that he meets my eyes.

His jaw sets, and he mouths, slowly, *"Don't. Move."*

My pulse quickens to the beat of a drum along with the hesitant nod of my head. My wide-eyed gaze shifts to the trees, the soldiers near me in the same position. Frozen, our breathing almost in rhythm as my heart pounds in my ears.

I glance back to Liam, alarm and confusion spreading through my every bone.

A twig snaps.

My head flinches to the right.

We fall, Liam's sweating hand enclosing around my wrist. He pulls before my body can resist, my hands slamming into dirt.

I catch a flash of dark brown before the ground swallows my glance, the heavy sound of something clomping in the dirt silencing us all. Quietly, I make it to my feet, my back hitting bark. I see Liam's face—steady, yet eager, as he glares through the trees to where the sound came from. His back is against a tree like my own, only a few feet away.

A bush's whisper prickles at my senses, rustling nearby. I can't help but lean further as my blinking eyes bend around the tree. Desperately and anxiously hoping to get a glance at the source of the unnerving sound, I ignore Liam's screaming eyes telling me to get back on the ground.

Dark brown was what I saw . . . and I see it more clearly, now in full, my fumbling lips parting like they're trying to make sense of what's before me.

A—a horse.

Not one, but two. More than two, perhaps three, except another one rustles the bushes as it emerges from the trees. Making it four.

My eyes trail upwards, past the body of the horse, and land on the body of a man, hard and tall. It's all I see, his broad shoulders covered by a green uniform. My head snaps back behind the concealment of the tree in sync with the chill shuddering down my neck and tingling my arms.

Eyes locking with Liam's, I dare to listen. Horse hooves stomp, a gruff voice sounding with a low rumble.

"Eh! Boy! Settle down now!"

A second, younger voice sounds, stirring my memory.

"Sir, the horses. They sense something."

"Well, aren't you bright?" The first voice spits out. "I can *see* they sense something, Tresting." Curses suddenly escape from the foul mouth.

My eyes shift from every inch of the ground to my hands and to my dress, to Liam. I frown at the second voice.

"Of course, sir."

My shoulder adjusts against the tree. Lip twitching at its corners. I edge to the right. My eyes squint, past the tree, and my heart skips a beat.

Warren. Irene's lad who sat on the barrel behind our house.

Tresting apparently is his last name. And for the life of me, I have no idea why he's on the top of a horse, dressed in that dreadful uniform. A dark helmet rests on his head, dark feathers, black as night, peaking at the top, changing the cowardly man who sat on a barrel against my porch walls into someone . . . dangerous. I can feel it by the hardening in his eyes as they study the branches above.

But then I do know why he's here, and it becomes clear, matching the same answer formed before, when I hardly had time to turn it over and over in my head. Warren's here in the forest because he's a traitor. And he's a traitor because these are evil men. Men that Warren must have led to my home to take Michael. I know about these men, and who they are, stories from Papa ringing in my ears, stories of encounters with their brutal actions.

Finally, a single name resonates in the deepest part of my mind.

Dragoons.

A stick thumps my leg, snapping my attention from the British men to Liam.

He raises a brow, landing his eyes behind me. I frown, hesitantly turning to peer over my back. The rest of the men begin to shift, gripping their gear. The four of them crouch, moving and stepping forward. I take in a steady breath and follow their lead, careful that the only sound made is my boots quietly sweeping through grass. My mind races. A burning anger, an ache, takes root in my heart at the thought of the blood on these men's hands.

Warren?

Warren is one of them, and a part of me is glad. Irene would never want to be with him now, but there are bigger things to worry about. If Warren is one of them, that means the British know . . .

And now it makes sense.

It was them. They did everything, all of the cannons, the attack, capturing Michael . . .

The Royal Dragoons are responsible for it all, and the man who was only feet away from my home just hours before was behind every horrific act.

10

STORIES FROM A MAJOR

THE SMELL INVADES THE camp. Raw meat cooking over small flames, smoke infusing the air.

The story from Papa plays over in my mind, as if it is happening right before me. It's about one of his long days among the tents and fires. His strides long and purposeful, he passes through circles of men. Men who have cheered and wept together. I hear Papa's voice tell of the details in each soldier's expression and the atmosphere of the crowded place. It feels like I'm back home, sitting in front of the fire with him, clasping my knees and studying his clear and full voice. He keeps my full attention with the way his voice rises and descends with emotion, matching that of his comrade's, sympathy glazed over his eyes. "Some soldiers laugh, somehow even in the darkest days," he says. "Some entertain. Others are silent . . . with tears from the loss of their closest friend taken in battle that day."

And it is this story, that the smells bring to mind all over again.

I quicken my pace to stay with Liam, our shoes stirring up dust. We've arrived earlier than Liam expected, the sun still visible on the horizon. I can see across the entire camp, lined with maybe thirty or more tents. Pots and pans, the odor of different soups or scraps cooking on the individual fires, it all blends together, chatter rising with the clanging of tools and tackle and such. I pull back to see behind Liam's shoulder, my eyes sweeping the other side of camp. Men. Tents. Fires. More men. All with a different story in their eyes.

My gaze centers on a soldier a few feet away, hat in hand, and I realize it's not the smell of sweat or meat over a fire that I notice. Those only stir my senses. The sight of the soldier's dirty hands as he grips and pulls at his hat, anything to fight the anguish from battle.

This is what stirs my heart.

"Are you excited to see your father?" Liam looks ahead, stiffened voice barely heard above camp's noises. The question catches me off guard, and I leave my mouth hanging as I stumble sideways, avoiding a soldier's boot. I gather the ends of my dress in a flurry of motion.

"Whoah there. Sorry, Miss."

I glance back over my shoulder to nod quickly and recover, catching up with Liam. His shoulders sway back and forth as he cranes his neck to the side to meet my eyes. He raises a brow, walking still.

"I'm fine." I glance back once more, the soldier lost in a blurry of smoke. I let the ends of my dress fall. "Um, yes, of course."

I follow the ground with my troubled gaze, frowning. "But this time is different. It's not just a reunion, you know? It's a meeting of sorts, to make a plan." My whisper reaches only his ears. "To get him back."

He only looks to me and nods, focusing narrowed eyes back on the tents all around. I look ahead. Liam acts so different. Focused. Serious. Of course, he must be thinking, going over what we encountered in the forest in his mind. What we are to do about it. Tugging on my arm's sleeve, I bring it around my stomach.

Could it really be? I study the fresh memory of a Royal Dragoon in my mind, his hardened eyes flashing, body rigidly tall on a striking beast.

Warren?

I turn to Liam, ready to disclose everything I know about Warren, as I haven't yet gotten the chance to, then movement to our side catches my attention.

Three soldiers roll dice along a plank of wood, involved in a lighthearted game of Farkle. I lift my head to see past them, watching a younger soldier, elbows resting on his knees as he watches the game with dreary eyes. He appears to be only a boy.

An ache tugs at my heart, reminded of the people these men, even those just past boyhood, had to leave behind.

Liam leads us off the main path through camp. My thoughts of the young soldier are forced to vanish as we approach a cluster of circular white tents surrounding one much larger. The main tent's flaps are open, guarded by a soldier on each side. I catch one of the guards glance, moving closer to Liam so that our arms are touching. I realize that the details about Warren will have to wait to be told.

"Peterson." Liam gives a smile that doesn't reach his eyes, clasping hands with one of the soldiers. "Hope you men are holding up well in this heat." Releasing the soldier's hand, Liam exhales, gesturing to the opened tent before the soldier has a chance to respond. "This is urgent, I'm afraid."

The soldier takes no time to pause, nodding firmly, holding the flap open wide. Liam moves to my side, tone quick. "Stay here." He motions to the soldier guarding the other side of the tent. "William will keep guard."

I almost protest to being kept from joining the conversation, but Liam turns briskly, disappearing into the tent before I can speak, followed quickly by the soldier he called Peterson.

The flap closes.

I slowly turn, facing the rest of the camp as a quick force of cool wind blows through, the temperature dropping with the setting sun. Just as slowly as the sun descends, an uneasiness settles in the pit of my gut. Everything is so foreign, so different. No matter the stories from Papa. How could they have fully prepared me for a day like this? I hug to my dress tighter, my glance flickering to the dark-skinned guard at the tent. I smile at him. A growl starts in my stomach, responding to the strong smell of meat infusing the air. Liam and his men had only a little dried jerky and hardtack to sustain us for the last twenty-four hours. When was the last time I had a full meal?

Before the attack . . . before the madness started . . . before there was even a reason to be at this camp. I scan the ground, blinking slowly, unable to get the image out of my mind.

Royal Dragoons.

They're the reason . . .

Of course, they are only a small part of this whole war. Yet they've stirred something in me not even Sarah has ever prompted. Is it hatred? Anger? The Bible says to not sin in your anger. So, is this a righteous anger growing in me?

I shiver at the thought of them, what they've done. How can I trust Liam's promise of Michael's protection when I now know who has him captive?

"*They won't kill him,*" Liam had said.

Anger races to my fists.

It's a lie. How could he make me believe that?
Of course they'll kill him.

I twitch at my fingertips. Perhaps this messenger is just kind hearted, attempting to calm my fears by convincing me they won't hurt Michael. Or perhaps he is a blind man, and cannot see these are ruthless, dark men. In which case, he would be a fool. Not that it should mean anything to me, either way.

Michael is still gone.

The flaps to the tent rustle as I whirl back around. They're thrown open, the soldier who went in with Liam rushing out as I dodge his shoulder. My eyes follow him, squinting through another breeze. He quickly makes his way towards a chestnut-colored horse, mounting. No soldier seems to notice as he rides out of view.

Is he a messenger like Liam?

I pull a strand of my braid out of the corner of my mouth, sighing aloud. Chatter in camp begins to soften, pink and orange starting to make a bonfire in the sky. Colors peek through the surrounding forest, just enough for me to catch their image and tuck it away in my mind, to remember their gentle flames.

The flap sounds with a whip to the side. I spin as Liam emerges, meeting my eyes, a look of frustration and even anger inside them. "We're sending scouts." Voice flat, he scans the area, grazing my arm as he passes. I turn as he walks, following him.

"That's—that's it?"

He stops short, blinking questioning eyes as I force patience out with my words. "Will we be doing anything else for my town besides sending scouts? What about sending enough troops to actually help?"

He tilts his head, glancing at the tip of my nose. "Nay, Miss Holt. Not yet."

I watch him turn, annoyed at him using my last name. He walks a few paces, back to searching the camp as my jaw sets, lips part. Wanting to shout at him, grab him, demand he explain. Suddenly he slows, standing still, as I move to his side.

"Until your father returns to camp tomorrow, sending scouts to gather information is all we can do."

He responds to my unconvinced expression. "It's the most important thing to do if we want to plan a successful rescue." His brow furrows in distress, matching the state of my heart and mind.

I shake my head, looking down. His eyes seem to soften when I look back up, shrugging wearily, searching his face. "How will we find him?"

He breathes in through his mouth, blowing out a deep breath.

"That's our next step. I promise."

My lips pinch, whisper a bit more brash than I intend. "You can't keep all of your promises, Liam."

The firmness in his gaze diminishes, and he smiles tiredly. "If I couldn't, I wouldn't be making them."

I inch closer, squinting up at him against the setting sun. "It appears you've got quite a lot on your hands in order to keep those promises then."

He grows still, tone hushed. "It appears so." His green eyes flash, reflecting specks of firelight from torches being lit around camp. There's a steadiness in his face as his expression changes and he swallows, so close I can hear the gulp.

Suddenly, I realize now's my chance to reveal Warren. Taking a breath, I glance at my hands. "I have something to tell—"

Our heads both snap to the side at a gruff voice calling out. Liam frowns, searching a face. I follow his gaze, finding a tall, bearded man approaching, his eyes on . . .

"Miss Holt!" The burly man, dressed in an officer's uniform, greets us with a wide-stretched grin, his hand extended. "Truly Miss, I cannot believe I am seeing you."

I meet his gleaming eyes, mouth opened. "Pleasure, uh . . ." Shaking his hand, I pause.

"Ah! Of course. Major Robert Brenley at your service." The officer's rosy apple cheeks blow out as he presses his lips into a smile.

"Robert Brenley!" Liam's voice raises with excitement. "Honestly sir, I never thought I'd see you again!"

My laugh comes out nervously as I glance over to see Liam grinning, studying the man with familiarity.

I stare at Liam, still shaking the stranger's, or, Major Brenley's, hand.

"Well, what then, did you think I would die in a battle with some pathetic redcoats? Ah, lad, you know me better than that!" Brenley slaps his hand against Liam's shoulder.

Liam's grin widens, and he dips his head almost jestingly.

"Sir, I do not think we have any say over how we spend our last breaths. It's just, I thought you were called back to the East, to join Washington's camp when they leave Valley Forge?"

"Aye boy, plans always changing." Brenley eyes him mysteriously. "The powers that be-knew a young lad with Irish blood like yourself needed an old brute like me in camp to keep you in line!" He continues, raising bushy brows, "Col. Holt sent me a letter, sending me this way to watch over camp at the news of marching Dragoons headed for this beautiful colony."

I catch Brenley's attention once he is still, my forehead creasing curiously. "Forgive me, Sir, but how do you know the colonel?"

He seems to hide a grin, though it doesn't do any good as he releases a soft laugh, amused. "I know your father well, dear. Even had dinner a right many times in your home when you were wee taller than a little lamb!" He bends over and measures with his hand in the air, barely two feet above the ground.

I have no remembrance of the Irish major, though I do vaguely recall from my childhood the loud laughter of Papa's guests around the dinner table.

"And your sweet mum."

My throat constricts.

Brenley pauses in reflection, looking hesitant to continue. "I had already returned to Ireland when she passed. A great loss to all, that was."

I stare at the ground, gripping the sides of my dress. The air seems suddenly colder. I tilt my head back up as the major continues, forcing my lips into a smile.

"Ah, your father told me you looked just like her. But he told only half the truth, as you are even more beautiful than she . . . and that's despite having your Da's nasty British blood!" He and Liam laugh together, enjoying a little Irish camaraderie at my ancestral expense.

My glance shifts just enough, seeing Liam study me faintly with pained-looking eyes. As if responding to my reaction I thought was unseen.

The first few years after losing Mother were the hardest, but it's not as difficult now. Only it's been so long since someone else has mentioned her. In no way could I have prepared for the fresh sting from Brenley's comments.

Silence breaks as Brenley takes a large breath. "And, of course, your father has told many stories of his brave Maddie!"

Looking up, I swallow sheepishly, only to glance downwards again. "Stories are his forte."

"Indeed," Brenley sighs aloud. "All of his soldiers relish his stories around the campfire, told late into the night." He looks from me to Liam. "He just makes them come alive. Especially the old stories from the Good Book, you know . . ."

A fond smile tugs my lips. "I didn't know he told those in camp."

I've grown up hearing the Bible stories from Papa, but I wouldn't have guessed he shared them with his comrades. But then, of course that's what Papa would do. He knows a story, he shares the story, when it serves a purpose. It's just Papa.

Brenley takes the next few moments to lead us to a tent, larger than the rest. A wooden table stretches out on the grass, filled with food and utensils better than any of the soldier's. My mouth gapes at the feast, walking to a chair as Liam takes a place on the end, Brenley on another side.

Several spoonfuls of beans are raised to Brenley's bearded mouth before story after story of his various battles and adventures with Colonel John Holt are told.

I chew on beef, listening intently. The stories make my heart wish for Papa's presence even more. "I'm sure he is grateful for you, Sir." I bring a pewter cup to my lips, sipping cider.

"Ah, I'm the grateful one, Missy." His burly hand runs down his beard, swiping away crumbs of bread. "Now tell me," Brenley takes a long breath as he turns my way and blinks lively blue eyes, "what would the colonel's daughter be doing in a place such as this? A place so improper for a young lady? I came all the way from Ireland to join this fight precisely so ladies like yourself could remain in the comfort of your home."

My glance flickers to Liam, back to Brenley. I crinkle the napkin in my hand, forehead creasing. "My town was attacked, Sir, by Royal Dragoons." Liam searches my face as I see him out of the corner of my eye, a look equally alarmed as perplexed written across his strong features. He studies his knife piercing a slice of chicken, silent.

He couldn't just be realizing it was the Dragoons who attacked River Springs, could he?

I swallow, continuing to Brenley, "I was brought here by Mr. O'Dally because of a letter from my father. My brother and the woman staying at my house with her daughter were supposed to escape with me, but . . ." My eyes cast downwards, a force of wind gusting through the tent, taking my words and carrying them away. I blink wearily at my half-empty plate. "Michael was taken, and Sarah and Irene escaped."

"My dear, that is awful." Brenley's voice peaks with shock. "You two let me carry on and on about days gone by when we should be moving to action to get that boy back?"

I look up to see disturbance burning in his eyes. It comforts me to know someone else cares about the state of my home and family. Maybe he can help?

He did say *Major* Brenley. Surely, he would have enough authority to order a rescue. "Liam, what have you done for this town? Have you sent help right away?" Brenley's face sets tight, shoulders straightened, as if he's now in control of protecting everything I know.

Liam reacts to the change in tone and mood, taking on more of the appearance that his title calls for. He pushes his empty plate to the side. "That's why we're here, Sir. We've just sent a scouting party to gather enough intelligence for us to plan a proper response upon Colonel Holt's return tomorrow." Liam scratches above his jaw, seeming to think through the day's events. He releases a frustrated sigh. "But Capt. Grover, argued that there were already too many attacks in Carolina that needed attention and I didn't need to waste my time on a common town such as River Springs." He spins a fleck of grass between his fingers, turning his lip in a scowl as he flicks it in the air. "The bloody fool."

Brenley conceals an angered laugh and nearly chokes on his drink, sitting up straight. "The bloody fool? Bloody fool my cup of cider! The man's a halfwit moron!"

I furrow my brow furiously, slamming my cup down suddenly. "*What*? Just who is this Captain?" I look from Liam to Brenley. Liam raises his brows, looking under a tightened gaze. I struggle to hide a seething glare. "A common town?"

Liam's brow snaps up at our reactions as he holds his cup, darting fierce eyes from me to Brenley in question. I clench my teeth and grip my fork, not regretting a word.

Brenley raises a finger in the air, wagging it side to side as my muscles relax. "We must be smart. Aye, the Captain doesn't have the brains nor balls to protect the men and women of any town, but there's nothing we can do about him now, children. We must direct our focus on how we can *act*!"

Brenley lifts his head, revealing a coy smile, and looks to Liam with a mischievous eye. "I'm beginning to see why John is so fond of you, young man. Much wiser to patiently plan a successful rescue based on reliable information, rather than rushing in half-cocked and wild eyed with revenge."

He grips his cup, swirling the liquid inside in circles.

I watch Brenley tip the cup to his lips, searching my thoughts. *So maybe Liam's calm, careful steps* are *better than my rush to action.*

Rising from the table and moving swiftly towards the opened tent flaps, Liam begins scanning the area. "They should have left by now, but I'd like to make sure."

Brenley relaxes back into his jovial self, wiping a napkin over his mouth. "They'll have you running this war before long, lad!" His words are partially obstructed by the drink and food he has finally turned his attention to.

Liam seems to barely hear the praise, continuing to search the camp for something. Or someone. Nodding to the major politely, I join Liam, curiously following his gaze from tent to tent. He stops with a jolt, apparently focusing on one particular tent with two soldiers standing at the flaps talking. Liam starts in the direction of the tent. "Something's not right."

I follow close behind without asking permission. A disturbance grows in my stomach at Liam's hurried strides.

"Simpson!" Liam calls out before we even reach the soldiers who talk in the remains of daylight. One of them turns as Liam inquires. "Why are you still here, soldier? The scouting party was supposed to leave immediately. We need that information back by first light!"

The startled soldiers quickly come to attention, surprised by Liam's barrage. "Lieutenant O'Dally, we, um, I—scouting party? I'm sorry, Sir, I have no idea what you're talking about."

Lieutenant? But he's just a messenger . . .

Liam leans forward slightly, honest surprise in his face. "Officer Peterson never spoke to you? He left the headquarters tent at least an hour ago."

Brenley approaches from behind, joining the confusion. "How long ago did you send the lad off?"

Liam and Brenley confer as I remember the soldier who first walked out of the tent, brushing past me in a hurry. His brooding face flashes in my mind. I frown, raising my voice to be heard by the men. "Liam? Who was the soldier that exited the tent before you did? Was that Peterson?"

He looks to the side, still surveying the camp with tension. "It was. Captain Grover sent him. I wanted to lead the party myself and take my men, but he insisted I stay with you," he nods my way, "until the colonel returns. I don't even know Peterson well enough to trust him with such a critical mission. He only transferred to our regiment a few weeks ago."

Now I understand Liam's frustration earlier as he emerged from the meeting in the tent. I inhale a ragged breath with a quickening heart rate. Slowly I shift my body around, facing the right side of camp. "Are the other members of the scouting party on this side of the camp?"

Liam looks up, nodding as he counts off tents. "Yes, all four of them are right here. Why?"

My lips part as I freeze. I shake my head forcefully. "Peterson went to the left. Straight to a horse and rode out of camp." Anxiety grabs my insides, my eyes leaping back and forth over Liam's as his face contorts.

"What?" His jaw flexes, though voice calm. "That's impossible. I gave him very clear orders."

"He went the opposite way, I'm telling you," I reinforce.

"Lad," Brenley catches Liam's attention with a hand on his shoulder and a knowing look, "if that soldier didn't take the scouts with him, then he went somewhere alone so no one else would know of his whereabouts."

The realization of the situation sinking in, Liam's frown spreads to his eyes, darkening his features. He raises a hand to the back of his neck, closing his eyes. "This is not good."

I look from Brenley to Liam, unnerved and troubled that for the first time in the few days I've known him, Liam O'Dally looks genuinely worried, even scared.

"Friends," Brenley squints up at the sky, sighing, "we just told a British spy everything we know about the colonel's town and sent him on his merry way . . ."

Liam stares hard at the dirt ground. "With a free pass to take that information back to his bloody redcoat friends."

11

A Hasty Departure

THE ATMOSPHERE CHANGES, SHIFTING from a day of travel into a night of unease as we quickly form a circle. Liam begins speaking faster than I can keep up, though with a sense of purpose that reminds me of Papa.

"A scouting party needs to be re-deployed immediately." Liam's hands move to his trouser pockets like I've seen several times before, calm and collected even in great alarm. "We have to find out more about Peterson, what other missions he's aware of." He nods to each of us gathered, a taut nervousness rising from the tiny group of just Brenley, Liam, the two soldiers, and myself. "Most importantly, where he's gone to. Tomah can track him," mid-sentence, Liam whistles a signal towards his squad's campfire, "and possibly even catch the traitor before he gets to wherever he's going."

Brenley nods solemnly. "We don't know any of this for sure, but we need to assume the worst for now. I'll speak with Grover and see if Peterson has been privy to any other critical information since he's been here." Liam turns back, nodding as Brenley directs the next comment to him. "You organize the scouting party and get them on their way."

Tomah jogs to our circle, a sheath full of arrows this time on his back, a beautifully carved bow over his shoulder.

Brenley turns to the skillful looking Indian. "Come with me, lad, to question Grover. Might find something out that will help you find Peterson. I'll fill you in on the way over to his tent." The two men are walking away even as Brenley wraps up his orders. Clearly the Irish major has had experience in this field.

"Major," Liam calls after forcefully, then shifts to a whisper, "what if Grover's in on it? He was the one that wanted to send Peterson instead of me."

Brenley raises those bushy eyebrows, tapping his temple with a finger. "Already ahead of you, lad. Been outthinking the Brits since before you were born!" His mouth stretches into a grin hiding mischief. "You leave Grover to me and your Indian friend here."

Liam turns back to me, determined with haste for action. "Your father returns tomorrow. You'll be safe here tonight in his tent. I'll be back by morning."

My response surprises me. "But the major only said for you to organize the scouting party, not go with them."

Liam takes a moment, seeming almost patient to explain as he looks down at me. "I know the way better than anyone. At this point, I'm not sure I trust anyone outside my squad." He raises a finger above his head, making a circling motion. I turn, watching Woods and Fields respond to the signal, having already picked up on the activity and starting towards us.

I spin back to Liam. "I need to tell you something, before you leave."

Hesitant to shake his head, he lets out an uncertain sigh. "Maddie, I'm sorry, there's really no time."

"It could be important if you're going back." I wait, watching him.

He glances to the side, looking on the soldiers and nodding quickly. "Hurry then, every minute counts now."

My pulse spikes as I recall the details about Warren. I scratch the bottom of my lip. "When we ran into Dragoons in the forest?"

He nods again, then holds up his hand with one finger as if to say, "one moment." He watches Kel join Woods and Fields as they prepare horses for the hasty departure. He calls after. "Kel! Fields! Find Tomah and go with him to track Peterson. Woods, you're with me. We ride for River Springs tonight." He pauses, looks back at me, then to them again. "I need a minute."

I jump right back in. "I know one of those Dragoons. I didn't know he was a Dragoon when he was at my house with Irene, but now I know. His name is Warren Tresting." I eye a soldier a few yards away who seems to be trying to overhear the conversation, or maybe now I'm just paranoid.

Still, I lower my voice. "He's been playing a suitor, fooling Irene."

Liam looks back to me and peers through the last bit of daylight. I shake my head in contempt at the situation. "Who knows what other tricks he's played, what information he's gathered. He could have been the main planner behind the attack." I look up at Liam, feeling vulnerable and embarrassed to share my weakness. "I didn't suspect a thing. I just thought he was entertaining a girl far too young." I can't help the frustration in my voice. "I'm such a fool."

"This isn't your fault." Liam searches my eyes, giving his head a few firm shakes to the side. "If he's who you say he is, then Warren was never going to allow you to figure him out." He looks to the side, watching the men. "You couldn't have done anything anyway."

Isn't he right? How would I have known? I swallow away a lump in my throat. "Just—watch out for him. Well, for any of them."

"Aye." He nods. He somehow makes everything more comfortable, and I release a long sigh, starting to feel the first signs of exhaustion that's been forced to stay at bay for the past few hours.

"I didn't think you would have even known they were Dragoons." He looks back at me. "I didn't tell you what I knew about them. Didn't want to give you more cause for concern." He smiles slightly. "I guess it's my turn to be impressed."

I allow myself a small smile back, being okay with not knowing what to say.

He breathes in, appearing to go over a mental checklist before he leaves. "I'll see that you're situated and then have William posted as a watch throughout the night. He's one of your father's personal assistants and even though he's not in my squad, I trust him." He shoots a wary glance to the side, chewing his bottom lip. "I think."

"That's comforting, *Lieutenant*."

He raises both brows. "Well, weren't you the one to say you wouldn't fully trust someone until you've known them for many years?" He allows a partial smile.

"Why didn't you tell me you were an officer?" I shake my head, stepping closer. "Why say you were only a messenger?" I know I'm keeping him too long, but it's our first moment alone since Simpson called him Lieutenant O'Dally.

His face and eyes soften, as if regarding me carefully. "Your father taught me that titles mean very little. It's what a man actually does that counts." As if on cue, his squad has mounted their horses and whistles impatiently to him that they are ready to depart.

Liam disregards them for a moment as he waives William over. "William, you saw Miss Holt earlier. Once she is settled in the colonel's tent, would you take watch over her for the night? He'll be returning in the morning. I need to check some things out and will be gone for a few hours." Liam's eyes tell me that we should guard information about where he and his squad are going.

"I'd consider it an honor, Lieutenant. The Lady will be safely looked after." More jovial than most soldiers, William gestures for me to follow him to Papa's tent.

Liam awkwardly shuffles between us. "Uh, I will do that for her." He turns to me, murmuring under his breath. "You're not walking through this camp alone."

I raise a brow challengingly. "But you just said William here—"

"I said he would watch the tent. I, and only I," Liam shoots a glance to William, "will escort you during your stay here." I notice the warning is sent to William more than me, so I close my mouth, watching the exchange.

"As you wish, sir. I didn't mean to cause a problem." William's brown eyes flash innocently, as if he isn't following Liam's concern at all.

Liam nods curtly. "Of course."

He runs a tanned hand through his hair. "Let's get you settled quickly."

My hand shoots over my mouth, covering a smile. William leads the way, nervously glancing back to confirm we are following him. Liam guides me slightly in front of him, hand on the small of my back. When did he decide to get so protective? I take a long stride, stepping out of Liam's reach as we pass rows of tents and fires. Doesn't he understand I don't need his protection all the time?

The evening grows heavier with darkened skies, the air cooling with the rising of the moon. Chatter dies down, men extinguish fires. "Here you are, Miss." William's nice smile and dark skin makes him a handsome young man. He opens the flaps to a medium-sized tent.

Offering a nod, I step over a peg on the ground, walking in with Liam and glancing back. "Thank you, William."

Liam lets the flaps close behind us, perhaps not meaning to rudely leave William out.

Or perhaps so.

The tent is somewhat cozy inside. Liam stays at the entrance, leaning half his weight against a long legged, wooden stand. He seems unsure what to do next, running his gaze around the tent's walls. "Very small."

I stifle a smile, my heart pricked by his concern. "It's perfect." I sidestep the wooden stand, sliding closer to him hesitantly. "Thank you . . ." My hand finds the stand behind me, supporting my weight. "For caring."

He interlocks his fingers at his bent waist, eyes dancing across mine. "You're welcome." He shuffles, obviously yearning to leave for the mission yet hesitating, perhaps unsure about leaving me alone.

I turn slowly, finger swiping across the stand and picking up dust. "When Papa gets here, everything will be alright." I smile, though my back faces him. "Then you won't have to watch me like a hawk anymore."

As I spin back around, he suddenly steps forward, locked on my face. My mouth turns dry for no reason as he blinks twice and inhales, as if about to say something. I sweep my eyes over him, hesitating—"I'll be fine, Liam. Go. Like you said before, we need good information before Papa can plan a successful rescue."

His back straightens and he lets out a slow breath, taking a small step back. "William . . ." He nods softly to the side, his eyes wistful. "He'll be sleeping right outside, ready to help you if anything should happen." Briskly he turns, pulling back the flaps with a peer behind his shoulder. "I ask that you not leave this tent until your father or I come for you."

I nod, moving with him towards the flap as he steps out. He stops outside the tent, smiling with his eyes. "Tomorrow."

My whisper is hushed by a soft breeze floating through. "Tomorrow." I keep his gaze, backing into the tent, forcing myself to let the flaps close. I stare ahead longer than I should, then turn to face the empty tent as a sudden sense of gloom falls around me.

The night seems lonely, and I am suddenly eager for the lieutenant's return.

12

And Angels Keep Watch

DARK SKIES PAINT THE cool night, brisk air brushing my cream-colored skin as I peek out the tent's flaps. A small fire glows warmly not far from my tent, the only light among camp. I bring my sleeves around my hands to battle the chilly night air.

How does it get this cold only a few hours after the heat of the day?

Not a sound is made throughout all the camp, only the chirping of critters puncturing the silence. Liam was not joking, William is curled up on the ground, sleeping right outside the tent. I quietly walk around him, intent on getting warm by that fire. I glance behind my shoulder, to the side, making my way. Shaking a strand of hair out of my eyes, I stop mid-stride, looking on a figure clothed in firelight. His sitting frame reflects dark shadows lining the dirt ground.

A chill runs across my arms, my brows drawing together tight. I make my footsteps quiet, leaning forward to study the stranger. A tricorne hat sits on his head. A long, black coat draping from his shoulders to the ground. His back rounds, elbows propped on his knees. The hunched shape looks very weary and spent . . . and familiar.

I walk to the side, staying at a far distance. Suddenly a part of me wishes Liam was at my side. The man's side profile comes into view, and I freeze in place.

Could it be?

I dare to inch closer, suddenly feeling a stick break under my shoe. The man whips around, hand flying to a knife at his waist. A familiar square jaw and black curly locks greet my gaze.

A force of emotion hits every fiber in me. My eyes well to the brim. My mouth drops, whisper hoarse. "Papa."

The blue eyes I haven't seen in so long, but have never forgotten, pierce through mine. His tall frame stands briskly, instantly. "Maddie . . ." Hearing his voice makes me fumble backwards. "Oh, Maddie."

I run like a small child. "Papa!"

His protective arms wrap around me, and I smell the combination of a long night's ride and forest dew. How could I have forgotten what it was like to hug him? I bury my head in his chest, tears spilling over my cheeks onto his wooly coat.

"Papa. Wha—what are you—" My lip quivers, stopping any words from escaping. I laugh unexpectedly, clutching him tighter. "I can't believe it's you! Liam said—tomorrow . . ."

Some say my Papa is as tall as General Washington himself, standing over six feet. I come to his chest, looking up to feel his smile warm away the cold. His blue eyes are serious yet adoring. Voice deep but hushed in the quiet camp. A wide hand brushes at my tangled hair. "Why are you out, my girl?"

I laugh into my sleeve. "I was headed for the fire . . . Oh, Papa!" I slip my hand into his, shaking it once. "There's so much to tell you!" Thoughts bombard my head, too fast for my lips to catch up. I grip him and widen my eyes, my voice urgent. "River Springs was attacked, raided by Royal Dragoons. Annie's was hit, and Michael!" I suck in a breath. "They took Michael! And Sarah and Irene, they just escaped—"

"Maddie!" Papa's hands move to my shoulders, his eyes wide with confusion. "What are you talking about? I thought Liam brought you all safely here to camp?"

The need to tell him everything quickens my heart rate, but my mouth opens only for me to fumble. "I—Royal—"

Papa's tanned face contorts as he leads me to the log by the fire. Immediately his eyes search mine as they seem to turn an even darker shade of blue. "Start from the beginning, child. Explain everything."

Fear grips my throat, and I raise a hand to massage a growing lump away. "I told you, Papa. Royal Dragoons. They attacked."

"Did you actually see them?" His brows knit.

I nod firmly. "Aye, Papa! Two Dragoons took Michael and the rest rode away. I never saw any actually raid the town because they were sheltered by the forest, but I know for sure what I did see." For a moment I stop breathing, feeling the dust coat my skin again. Gusts of smoke and the replay of a torrent of screams seem to flood my eyes and ears. I wrap my arms around the rest of my body, looking to him. "Royal Dragoons."

Papa's head tilts slowly in the light of the fire. He appears suspicious as he studies me and leans in. I watch him and continue at his silence, closing my eyes to recall. I feel my legs clench, remembering the burn of them running. "So much was demolished, debris and fallen shops everywhere. I had run as fast as I could, I tried to save him, I promise, Papa." A memory flashes in my head while I look into his gaze, Michael's curly head beneath two soldiers as he struggles against their hold. The same defeat that pushed me against Liam's shoulder while Michael was still being held behind tumbles over my lips. "But I didn't save him. I couldn't. I'm so sorry, Papa."

For a moment, I'm not sure that he believes me. But he grows still and his eyes stay unblinking as his forehead creases in deep thought. "What kind of soldiers would take a child like Michael?"

I hide my surprise at his response. No emotion lies in his eyes or panicked questions on his mouth. He is quiet and pensive, unreadable and unmoving. "Dragoons, like I told you." I furrow my brow, impatient.

"When? When did it happen?"

"Just yesterday," I hurry, glad to finally have his attention. "I had just met Liam in the woods, and he gave me the letter. But after I came back home to gather my things, the cannons went off—"

"You must have seen regular redcoats," he stops me, watching the ground as if stuck on a previous thought. "Dragoons are an elite, often rogue band of ruthless mercenaries and they don't operate this far southwest—"

"I know what I saw, Papa!"

He leans in on his knees. "What did the soldiers look like?"

"They aren't soldiers," I let out, shaking my head. "They're criminals." The image of their green vests and red jackets resurface, two pairs of arms pulling at Michael. "Michael was grabbed by men dressed just like Dragoons." I look up to him. "Just like the one's you've described in your stories. Green vests. Feathers in their helmets."

He gives a quick nod, as if he is accepting the truth of who they really are. Another quick nod, as if Papa has already made a decision and has a plan. "Which direction did they take your brother?"

The word brother stabs every muscle, every fiber in me, and I grow tired of his interrogation. The question brings on a queasiness, making me dizzy. I close my eyes and reach back to recall the details of that horrid day.

"They . . ." A picture of our wooden house shows up in my vision. "To the left our house, if you're facing the front." My eyes open, shifting to him. "Into the woods."

Papa stares hard at the dirt ground, appearing unwilling to answer. Perhaps reconsidering whether he is willing to accept the news.

I want to say something more, raise a hand to his shoulder. But I also want to cry. Lean into his shoulder rather than pat it, because I can't sit up any longer. I look over and catch my breath, following the tear trickle down my father's cheek with weary eyes. He sniffs, folding his hands, elbows propped on his knees. "Where's O'Dally, dear?"

I hide my surprise at the question, shifting on the log. "He . . . well, that's the thing. He's not here." I blink drearily, having almost no strength left to argue. "Why? I can tell you everything he could about the attack."

He lifts his brow through a teary gaze, dubious. "If he's not here, then there must be a very good reason for him to leave you with so many soldiers you do not know."

I hold his stare. "I know William."

He leans in with a tired smirk tugging at his mouth, despite the seriousness of the situation. "Yes, well, William is a good lad, but Liam is the one I wanted watching over you."

I inhale a deep breath and frown. "There *is* a reason Liam's not here, that's what I've been trying to tell you. He took a group of soldiers to survey town, where the Dragoons attacked."

He's silent, as if a lump in his throat keeps him from opening his mouth, choking out any possible word. If there are even any words to say. I've said all I can . . . everything's now left to Papa to decide.

"What about Sarah and Irene?" His head lifts suddenly.

I pause, dreading even thinking about the two. So there *is* more to say.

Papa has never been around enough to actually spend time with the two women he took in, but he obviously cares about them and their well-being. Sarah was widowed before asking Papa for a roof over her head in exchange for being the caretaker of Michael and me. Having pity for her and her daughter, he made sure they were sheltered from that day forward and even now he feels a sense of responsibility for them.

Except that Papa can't do anything about them now.

I hurry to explain, not feeling a bit of relief for the fortunate events. "They escaped in time. Ran into the forest. Probably better off if something happened to—"

"Maddie," his weary snap silences me. I look further away. "Do not wish harm on innocents."

Wouldn't we be well-off without them? Sarah never cared for any of us. Now I see that her only obvious intention was to marry Papa for recognition. My mouth clamps shut, though thoughts run through my head rapidly, one after another, wishing they could be said.

Sarah never actually cared, all those times Papa was gone. She never thought anything of us, from her strict rules to demanding voice, her unfair treatment of providing more food for Irene than Michael.

Papa should have known . . .

"No one could ever replace Mama." I only realize I whispered the thought after Papa looks at me, wide eyed.

I glance down, cheeks red.

He clears his throat and lowers his gaze, seeming to let the comment go. His voice remains a whisper as his head stays down. "Michael . . . you're sure?"

The silence steals the air for itself, tightening my throat. I move a hand to my stomach, clenching rough material, barely managing a hoarse whisper. "Yes."

My hands wring in my lap, a dewy mist descending upon grassy land, clouding the air around us. Trees sway in the distance to their own song . . . though if you forget yourself for a moment, and open your heart, you can hear it along with them. I blink my eyes drearily, wishing to get up and disappear to the forest, to dance and pretend none of these last two days were real.

Papa's hands drop as his gaze turns to the fire. I study him for a moment and realize I haven't helped anything at all. The weight of his whisper seems to make the air colder, the night heavier.

"They took my little boy?"

Surprisingly the ache has lessened, and I want to snap. Scream at something. I tighten my fists into a ball. "Haven't you been listening, Papa?" I look around, as if pleading with at least the trees to hear me, but finding no response. My throat grows thick and my mouth turns dry as I dart my glance from the darkened sky to the ground. I hug my waist, sitting still.

Will the morning ever come? What if from now on, even the mornings awaken the anguish of Michael's capture to my heart and mind? The night stills around us, understanding that now is a solemn time.

Suddenly Papa rises, looking down. "I need you to help me."

I shoot up, eyeing him. "Yes—of course, Papa. Anything."

He extends an arm. "You can help me by getting sleep tonight, and then assisting me in mapping out a picture of everything you saw that day at sunrise."

I shake my head quickly. "I can't sleep now. Not with Michael still missing and Liam gone for the night."

Papa pauses a moment just long enough so that the silence is uncomfortable, as if he's reading me. "Then you might as well help me form a picture of what happened."

A smile stretches across my face. I nod firmly.

"Come over here, to the dirt." His voice is still quiet in order to not wake the other soldiers.

We crouch to our knees, finding sticks.

He points to the ground with the pointed end of the piece of wood. "I need you to outline for me every place the cannons fired from. Can you do that for me?"

I nod hesitantly, then more firmly after painting in my mind the picture of town on that terrible day. Swiftly, my hand goes to work, fingers lightly gripping the stick like they would a paintbrush. I forgo outlining the front of town, and work on making a scribbly tree line and a row of shops towards the back. "I can't say for sure where the first one came from. I was inside." I nod, thoughtful. "But once outside, I know for sure they came from here . . ."

I point to one drawn square.

Papa lowers his head to look closer, rubbing his scruffy chin. "How long between cannon shots?"

"Not long, definitely not enough to have moved the cannons. I think they were all fired from the same spot, at least while I was there."

I designate four spots where the cannons hit their targets, remembering Annie's being hit and another small shop close to the spot we had knelt, surrounded by clouds of dust. I raise the stick, my wrist curved in the air, satisfied with the illustration once finished.

"You're sure this is where the canons fired from?" Papa points to a square drawn in the dirt.

"Yes, Sir. It hit Annie's." My lips curve downward in a frown, remembering the horror that coursed through me at the sight of Annie's wall tumbling down with a crash.

"Annie's? Was she there? Was Lydia?"

"Only Annie, and she seemed mostly okay, but very shaken up."

Papa nods deeply, eyes narrowed on the circle at our feet. With his stick, he taps the back of the circle, lined with scribbles of trees. "If the Dragoons started firing here like you said, then they came in from the west." He pauses, his head shaking slightly. "We had it all wrong."

I furrow my brow and wait. What does he mean?

Frustration, mixed with regret, lines his forehead and glazes over his blue eyes. "We were sure they were marching in from the east and our reports said they were regular soldiers."

I glance back to the dirt, running through my thoughts. "Papa, Dragoons are cavalry . . . they would have arrived at their destination before you were able to find them out. As long as you thought it was just regular redcoats approaching, you didn't expect them for several more days." I pause to think on the new idea. No wonder Papa kept insisting I saw redcoats and not Dragoons . . . redcoats were who he was expecting, not highly trained, elite British troops who covered miles on their resilient mounts faster than any other soldiers in either the British or American Army.

"Aye." He turns to me with a glean in his eye. "When did you get so smart, dear one?"

I smile up at him. "Great teachers raise great students." Leaning into his shoulder, we lower to sitting positions on the ground.

After a moment Papa's deep, gentle sigh vibrates through my head laid against his chest. "I need to speak with Robert Brenley. Has he arrived?"

"Liam and I spoke with him today." I lift my head, glancing behind my back. "I'm not sure which tent is his."

"I'll call on him in the morning. You need to sleep while the night hours are still here." Papa rises and leaves the stick on the ground.

"But Papa, there is so much more to tell you." My words start spilling out, not making much sense even to me as I rub my eyes wearily. "A spy, Peterson, from this camp, and Liam thinks maybe Captain Grover too. And Warren, he's a Dragoon but was on our back porch with Irene—"

"Shhh, child, I think your first time in a soldier's camp and the lack of sleep is playing games with your mind. Get some sleep and we'll sort it all out with Brenley at first light."

Weariness makes my eyelids ten pounds heavier as I nod in reluctant agreement, taking his hand that lifts me onto my feet. "I'll show you our tent." My words jumble together as a yawn widens my mouth.

"You go ahead. I will know which one it is." He looks up to the midnight sky, scanning the trees that sway to a cool breeze. "I'm going to stay out for a bit longer. Pray to the Lord for wisdom."

I watch the branches dance with him, just barely seen by the firelight. The night is still, the air is crisp, the cream moon full. I breathe in deeply to remember it all, and stumble into Papa's chest like I did only moments earlier. Again, I relish in the fact that my Papa is here, and I am held by him once more.

"Let the angels keep watch tonight, my Maddie." He brushes the top of my hair with a kiss, hugging me firmly and fondly all at once, just like he would every day at home. My eyes flutter shut, wanting him to say it again. The words he would speak to me every night as a child, up to every night before he left, words that soothed my mind and quieted my worries. The angles will keep watch tonight . . .

Sleep will come, and peace is here.

I release him and step back, smiling up at his scruffy face. "Goodnight, Papa." My eyebrows lift. "Please come to the tent soon. I hate to be away from you now that you're here."

He strokes the top of my head, eyes reassuring. "I promise."

I nod, stepping away from the warming fire, turning on my heel to look back once more. "I love you, Papa."

He seems to choke on some unknown emotion, silent for a moment. "I love you too, dear Maddie." He shifts, lifting his hat to swipe a hand over his forehead. "Get some rest now."

I let a smile fall on my lips as I pull up the ends of my dress so as to not trip on anything in the dark, turning to face the rows and rows of tents. I find the large tent hastily, quick to get out of the cold and under the wool blankets. Wrapping both sleeves around my waist and the thick blankets over my chin, I pray before drifting off to sleep.

Liam comes to mind, the dangers he could be facing in the night, and even more once morning comes. I beg God for his divine protection, surprised in the middle of my prayer at my deep focus on the young messenger. Suddenly aware of my fervent concern for him, I let my prayers shift direction and praise God for bringing Papa back to me, or bringing me to him, however it went about. No matter, my heart still overflows with joy this night.

Yes, Michael is gone.

Yes, these circumstances are impossibly hard.

But now, under this tent, dwelling on the faithfulness of God, the same God who split the Red Sea so His chosen people could walk right through it, I surrender my heart to peace and let my eyes close, and the angles keep watch tonight.

13

Ransacked

THE CHIRPING BIRD OUTSIDE my tent wakes me up to the morning. My heavy eyelids struggle to open, a stretch forming from my hands to my legs. A peak of sunlight spies through the tent's flaps, forcing my head back under the warm concealment of the blankets. A smile settles on my lips as I realize all that happened last night.

Papa's back.

Commotion sounds outside, the stomping of horses and shouts of soldiers. A young, male voice shouts, probably William just outside my tent, excitement filling his announcement. I yawn contently, casually listening and closing my eyes again.

"Lt. O'Dally is back! Someone find Col. Holt!"

Liam!

My eyes shoot open, the blankets flying off my legs and to the side. I stumble off the cot and crash to the ground. I groan, rising most ungracefully to a full stance. Taking a moment, my head finally clears and I eye the pitcher of water on a stand nearby. Gripping its handle, I down most of it's contents and swoosh a large amount around to rid the tacky morning texture in my mouth. I use the last bit to splash onto my face, rubbing away another one of morning's evident effects that settled around the eyes. After drying my face, I smooth down my hair, running my hands over my wrinkled dress, and tie on my shoes.

The sun is already warming the day as I step out of the tent. Immediately, chaos surrounds my every angle as I dodge two soldier boys running at full speed. I squint under the sun's glare, stepping around my tent and searching for Liam and Papa. Noticing the group of soldiers making their way towards the entrance of camp, I step in line with them, holding the ends of my two-day old dress. My head and neck strain to see around and between the men, catching sight of the heads of horses. The group spreads out, each approaching a horse and some taking the reins, ready to bring the horses to a place of shade. My eye finds the rider of the one closest to me . . .

Woods!

I grin, stepping past the other soldiers, trying to get his attention. The young soldiers taking care of the horses have no idea where the men have been, they simply focus on the task at hand without any urgency. It's my town that is in danger and my brother that is gone. My heart can wait no longer, fearing a grave report is about to be given. I want to find Liam, but with Woods so close, there's no reason not to hear it from him.

Finally, close enough to be heard, I raise my voice above the commotion. "Woods!" I rise on my tiptoes, pushing past shoulders. "Woods!!"

His head snaps my way, catching my glance. "Miss Holt!" He swings a leg over his saddle, hopping down. A young soldier takes his horse's reins, leading it away from the crowded circle.

I catch my breath from the long walk, offering a smile. "Praise God for bringing you all back." He offers a tight hug in response as I speak over his shoulder. "Tell me, what of my town?"

His brow furrows in as he pulls back, and he bites hard on his lip. "Perhaps . . . The lieutenant should be the one to tell you, Miss."

I swallow hard, not allowing a pit of nervousness to take up residence in my stomach. I close my eyes, forcing deep breaths in and out through my nose. "Is it that bad?" As I open my eyes, Woods raises a hand to my shoulder, giving a regretful smile and lowering his gaze. He walks with the other soldiers towards camp, leaving me with no news of my town.

Why couldn't he just say it? Doesn't he know I've been waiting, in torment of all the possible scenarios, for a report? Doesn't he know I've been praying through the night that the news would be good and the people at home would be safe?

Three horses in front of me stomp away, led by more soldiers, revealing only one horse and its rider in the open grass, cleared of the large group that was there just moments before. My eyes find a piercing green stare settled on mine.

I come up to Liam's horse, patting the strong steed on its white, thick neck. Liam's smile comes forced, I notice, but the grave state of his face doesn't diminish the usual bright flicker in his eyes. He swings a leg over the saddle just as Woods did, though quicker, more agile. I notice his skin pale slightly as he lands a few inches from me and wraps the reins in his hand around his palm. "Good morning." His tawny-yellow hair clings to his sweaty face in damp clumps. He wears the same white shirt that he did the first day I met him, a few new holes now ripped through the material.

"Good morning." My smile widens. "You're back sooner than I expected."

His head cocks as he inches closer, and his eyes have less of a gleam than I remember from the previous day. "How are you?"

"Alright . . . I think." I fold my ankles over one another. "It depends."

He raises both brows. "You want to know of your town."

I nod calmly, waiting. Realizing I should make it clear that I'm thrilled for their safety, I search his eyes once more. "I'm glad you and the men are safe. I prayed non-stop."

"Thank you. Really." He searches my eyes, a loose smile stretching across his face as he pulls the reins to the horse. "Will you come with me to find your father? Then I will explain all that I saw while at your hometown. I'm sorry to make you wait, but I'm afraid I've barely enough left in me to give this report once."

We fall in step together on each other's side, a refreshing breeze blowing through camp as we walk.

"I haven't seen Father this morning, but he's possibly with Mr. Brenley. Perhaps in the meeting tent with other officers."

"I'll put Gideon up first, then," he motions to the lean horse.

We find a place of shade with the other horses just as William fins us. "I'll take him, sir." The soldier strokes the horse's white mane. "The colonel is waiting for you in the Headquarters tent."

Liam nods his thanks, relieved to be turning over the reins, then motions for me to follow with a sluggish hand. Even in his physically weathered state, I have to lengthen my strides to keep up with his. I grip the ends of my dress, quickening my pace and wiping hair out of my eyes. The auburn locks cling to my back in the heat without being in a braid.

"Your hair—" Liam peeks from the side.

Maybe he is just exhausted, but to me he sounds reflective and kind. "Down like that, you look . . . older."

"Oh—" Still, I pause, not quite sure how to respond. "Thanks."

He grins, looking back to the path ahead of us. "My mother had auburn hair."

I press my lips together, wistful. "My mother did too. Michael and I both got her hair. But we got our eyes from our father."

"I can tell." He clears his throat, looking ahead. "Ocean blue."

I bite down on my lip, staring a bit too long. We approach a tent larger than the rest in camp all too soon.

"This is it." Liam steps ahead, nodding at two soldiers. They stand at attention, pulling both flaps back. Liam nods, motioning me inside. I duck my head and enter. Crowded around a wooden table strewn with maps and papers, soldiers shuffle and fill the grassy area with serious conversation. I don't recognize the men, besides Major Brenley and . . .

Papa.

I rush to his side, leaving Liam, still not used to the fact that I can be with Papa again. He kisses the top of my head, smiling gratefully to Liam who straightens and looks to the rest of the men in the room. The arrival of the awaited messenger silences every voice.

Liam raises a hand to his forehead, saluting. "Col. Holt, I've come straight from River Springs. I apologize for interrupting, but I think you will want this report immediately."

One of the other officers, a short man with a long blonde beard, nods enthusiastically. "Yes. Please do report, our other matters can wait."

"Excellent. If you all would allow—"

"Now hold on youngster." From the back of the tent, an elderly man with hair pure white and a frame fragile as a stick emerges from the group of a half-dozen men. I lean further into Papa, studying the old man. He must be of high rank, by his starch blue jacket and golden tassels on his front pocket. I'm not sure which rank they stand for, but by his commanding presence and the way every soldier turns his way, he must be vital to the war. I peer up quietly and am taken aback at noticing a small scowl under Papa's lips. He eyes the man warily, as if wishing the last thing on earth for him was to be under the officer's command. I try not to laugh when I catch Major Brenley rolling his eyes at the self-important man.

"Would it not be appropriate," the man starts, "to have this poorly dressed gentleman introduce himself to these men of the American Army itself?" He clicks his tongue, running beady eyes over the group. I pray the Lord keeps them from landing on me. "Hardly respectable for one so young to stand in the company of those who surpass him in years and not honor their presence first." The man presses his lips together in a satisfied, tight smile that does anything but flatter his already crinkled face.

I expect Liam's cheeks to redden and his lips to fumble, or perhaps his anger to boil. I hold my breath, waiting to see how he will react, and witness the exact opposite of what I expected.

He looks to the other men, brows raised, and back to the old man with a half-smile. "I apologize for any lack of respect from my haste, Sir. How tragic for an officer in the American Army itself to not introduce himself to his comrades." Liam's spine straightens.

I freeze, realizing the loaded response Liam just made. Wittingly and stealthily, he reminded the grumpy man of Liam's own position in the army, while also showing respect to the higher-ranking officers in the tent. He's every bit a part of this war as the others. Perhaps the man assumed he was a hired spy, but surely now he will not question him or his intentions.

"General Smeed," Papa interjects, "this is one of my most trusted officers and I'm sure he meant no disrespect."

Liam continues, stepping forward daringly and gesturing to his ripped pants and shirt. "I apologize for my poor attire, for I have just come back from an overnight mission in the service of our beloved country. My men and I have been riding all night to get the information we knew Col. Holt would be anxious to receive." There is nothing joking in Liam's tone, and his gaze settles resolvedly on the man as the general's countenance changes from lofty and superficial to slightly embarrassed.

I hide a proud smile, impressed by the way Liam handled the insults. Peering up once again, Papa's eyes narrow even harder on the older man and I feel his fist clench at my side. What does he not like about this General Smeed? Besides his irritatingly haughty attitude, of course.

With that, the man's mouth clamps shut, and he regards Liam with a look of hate so strong that it sends a shiver down my skin. My aggravation rises, jaw clenching, as I wonder who could ever treat a soldier as Liam in such a way. This man should be home in his bed, humiliated, while his fellow men go off to fight for honor and victory.

My lips curl and I turn my attention back to Liam, who inhales a breath and is looking at me. He shakes his head, dancing vexed eyes over mine. I nod confidently, urging him to go on. His hands clasp behind his waist, and I realize that he's taller than the majority of men here as my eyes run over the rest of the group, ears opened to Liam's comfortable and inviting voice.

"Gentlemen. My thanks for allowing me to join in this meeting. I am humbled. I'm afraid what I have to share is very grave after scouting River Springs."

Looking back, I see Liam's gaze shift, landing on mine.

I grip Papa's arm with a sweating palm, every muscle and bone tensing.

Grave?

At this moment, I'm too stiff to pray, too fearful in heart and mind of the report to come. My eyes close tightly, and I suddenly wish to be anywhere else, with Michael safe at home.

Liam's voice does nothing to comfort me this time, but only makes my body go rigid so that my knees lock and I grow lightheaded. I struggle for a breath, staring Liam down hard, as if willing him to say something good.

Anything. Any news of Michael. Please . . .

Liam takes no moment in pausing, shifting his weight to one side and meeting eyes with each person smart enough to look at him while he speaks.

My heart stops as his mouth opens.

"The town was ransacked. At least half the buildings in town were destroyed by the canon fire. Several were killed, even more injured. The only doctor in town is overwhelmed and frankly, in over his head and barely coping with the situation." The room is silent, no one knowing if that is the full report.

"The good news is that the British did not attempt to hold the town and no troops remain in River Springs." A collective sigh of relief passes over the group, the silence once again broken by the haughty officer who challenged Liam.

"Well then, this does not sound like a serious enough matter to keep our attention, we've much more weighty issues to deal with." No one seems to want to challenge the man. They begin shuffling back around the maps and papers spread across the large table in the center of the tent.

Liam is staring at the ground, barely noticing the others in the room, his voice eerily quiet, as if he does not want to share what he has seen. "That's not the worst of it. The Dragoons executed five men of River Springs right in front of the rest of the townspeople."

A gasp rises from the group at the mention of Dragoons.

I look around, glance frantic and surprised that these men didn't guess who were our attackers. Liam seems to be over them too, focused only on Papa and me. His gaze falters, eyes unable to be read so that I can't tell if he's speaking the truth or not. Because what

I'm hearing, no way . . . there is no way this could be true.

God would not allow this.

Liam inhales a shagged breath and every hint of resolve, every morsel of courage I've seen in him withers into nothing but exhaustion and defeat. His loud sigh is frustrated. "There is no sign of any of the remaining men from the town, other than the doctor, who gave me most of this information. I do not know if they are being held captive somewhere, or . . . or if they were all killed in addition to the public executions."

"No—" A groan escapes my trembling lips before I can stop it. Tears flood my eyes as I grip onto Papa, forcing my head into his chest. A name I wish wouldn't pop into my head enters all my senses, so that I begin to believe I'm hearing it whispered in my ears.

Uncle Henry . . . Uncle Henry . . .

14

UNWAVERING

MY MIND RACES WITH POSSIBILITIES, and the thought arises that if they executed those men, then why wouldn't they do the same to Michael?

My heart rate increases, breaths uneven. Papa's gentle hush does nothing but force me to silence as I peer out of his coat. I find Liam through a blurry lens and bite my lip to stop the pain.

He's approached the long table, elbows propped on the surface and head in his hands. I just need him to look at me . . . then I will know if it's true. I think I whisper his name, but with a voice so weak, who can hear me? Only my thoughts can be heard now, and only by One. But is He even listening anymore?

I push the thought aside, trying to focus on Liam and what he said. Another thought comes to mind—this time, small hope with it.

If they did kill every man, then why capture Michael? They would have just killed him on the spot if that was their intentions. Maybe there is still hope . . . maybe they are keeping Michael alive, and if so, there's a chance of rescuing him.

The small possibility does much for my soul and weaves a tiny thread of faith. Liam's head remains down, and I want to scream at him to look up, to let me see him. Papa approaches him authoritatively, voice strong, yet still kind. "Liam . . ." He pauses, as if expecting him to look up at his voice. When he doesn't, he seems to withhold a sigh. "Please. We need to know everything. Was there any sign of Michael? Do we have any idea why they chose River Springs?"

Liam's voice is cracked and faint, muffled by his palms. "Col., perhaps I should share the rest in private with you?"

"Not as long as I'm the highest-ranking officer here!" General Smeed suddenly steps forward, an obvious intent to take over the conversation in his face and tone. "You will reveal everything you know about this situation for this entire company and you will do so at once!"

Papa steps between Smeed and Liam. "That's enough, general. You are here to observe and advice. General Washington made it very clear that this regiment answers directly to me, and you may not interfere in the chain of command. If Lt. O'Dally has information he deems too sensitive for this group, I am inclined to hear him out privately first. We've already found one spy in our camp, my son has been captured, my home town attacked, and my daughter barely escaped. So, if you don't mind, *general*," disdain drips from Papa's lips, "your services are not needed at this time."

The general's face looks as if it will explode. He stares at Papa, considering a challenge, but after a huff or two and facial contortions the likes of which I've never seen, he suddenly calms and attempts to regain his pride as he strolls out of the tent. "These matters are too trivial for my time anyway. Anderson, step lively son." His aide quickly follows and the rest of the group files out, leaving only Papa, Liam, Brenley, and myself in the tent. The absence of the men leaves a short silence lingering in the air, almost immediately followed with the belly laugh of an Irishman.

211

"Well, that right there was worth leaving my beloved Ireland!" Brenley's grin reveals how much he loved the entertainment. "To see a colonel put a general in his place without court martial, and for it to be more deserved than any exchange I've seen on this continent . . . I can die a happy man now!"

Papa is not so amused. "He's a general in name only, Brenley. Smeed is nothing but a peacock in a uniform. He has no actual authority and was only given the title because Congress was thanking him for his financial donations to the cause. Enough of this. Liam, tell us what you know."

"Col., this is all about you, not River Springs. The executions were made because those men refused to share any information about you or your family, which appears to be the sole reason for the invasion." Liam cocks his head, sniffing. "Sir, why were they so focused on you? What if you are their main target?" As he looks at the colonel, I notice that his eyes seem to have lost some of their green.

I shake my head as Papa shifts next to mine. "I don't care about myself. Michael must be rescued. Perhaps they would be willing to make a trade?"

"Not a chance. No way will I stand for that." Brenley disagrees. "You don't even know why they want you yet. We need more information." He turns back to Liam, "Lad, were you able to find out anything about where they are holding Michael?"

Liam swallows deeply, blinking bloodshot eyes over at me and nodding back to Papa. "No, sir. They did a good job of covering their tracks just outside of town."

I can't stay silent any longer. "Liam, what about when we crossed paths with the four Dragoons? Doesn't that tell us which direction they were headed?"

The messenger is surprised, maybe even impressed.

"That's certainly thinking like a soldier. But unfortunately, those men were headed back towards River Springs for whatever reason, though there was no sign of them last night or this morning."

Liam swallows deeply, blinking bloodshot eyes over at me and slowly shaking his head side to side as he turns back to Papa. "We have no idea where the Dragoon camp might be, or even if that is where they are holding Michael." The scratchiness in his voice almost makes me gasp.

A feeling of hopelessness falls over our group. The silence in the tent is deafening until we each slowly notice that Liam . . . is . . . falling?

Brenley barely reaches out in time to catch him, and I gasp at the green tint to Liam's cheeks, covering my mouth. I walk over calmly but quickly. Instinctively, as I would with Michael, I place the back of my hand to Liam's forehead. Feeling hot warmth scorch like a flame underneath my hand, I tighten my brows and motion to Papa. "He has a terrible fever." I keep my voice hushed.

Papa's eyes squint, his sigh pained. "Let's get him to a tent. You'll watch over him while we start planning the counter attack." Brenley retrieves two soldiers from outside while Papa guides an arm around Liam's side, waiting for help. "He'll recover faster if he has someone taking care of him. We need him back in the fight as soon as possible."

"Yes, Papa." I nod, studying Liam's limp frame and feeling anxiety grip my stomach.

Two soldiers come and wrap both arms around Liam's upper body as Papa takes his lower. I bite my lip, praying that it won't take long for the color to come back into the lieutenant's eyes.

***

Inside the tent is only a wool blanket lining the ground, a wooden stand to the side holding a pitcher of water, and a rag. A white linen cloth lies on the blanket, wrapping scraps of food inside, and I already decide that they will go to Liam. I carefully remove his shoes without waking him after the solider behind me props him up with an extra blanket. I turn to the soldier. "Could you find extra blankets for him tonight, Sir? It's sure to get cool quickly and he needs to sweat out this fever."

The soldier nods, setting off to find the supplies. I turn slowly, a bit unsure of what to do next.

Liam has fallen asleep, breathing fast and shallow with sweat dotting his forehead. Chewing on the inside of my cheek, I lower to my knees, running a tentative gaze over him. I've never had the chance to truly observe him, but I feel uncomfortable doing so. I can imagine he would be uncomfortable knowing a girl was inspecting him while he sleeps.

Yet still, I can't help but notice the structure of his face. Strong cheekbones, defined sharply by curving inwards towards a pair of flushed lips. Reaching fingertips up to graze my jawline, I realize it is square, like his. His eyebrows are thick and darker than his hair, which is held back loosely by the same black ribbon it's always held in. I wonder if he's ever considered cutting it during the summer heat. Perhaps he just likes it this way.

And his eyes are green, I would confirm for another time, if his eyelids were open. I'd will them to not be bloodshot and tired, but fiercely alert and mischievous, as they should be. I feel a sigh rise in my chest and release slowly as my knees slide further to the ground. I sit on my bottom, hand dropping, coming to rest by my waist.

"Maddie!" A harsh whisper comes out of the tents flaps. I whip around, greeted by Papa's urgent gaze. I stumble to my feet, trying to grab a fistful of the tent's tough material, but coming up short and nearly falling over as I rise.

Papa's brow furrows in at me and his mouth opens and closes. "Maddie . . . listen."

I finally regain my footing, shooting up straight. "What—yes, hi Papa." I slide a strand of hair out of my mouth, raising my temple with widened eyes. "What is it?"

He holds his breath and searches my eyes, as a father would who just stumbled upon their child doing something they could not understand. He finally moves, beckoning with his hand. "Come outside." Stepping from the tent, he reveals glaring sunlight. "I'm going away tonight with a group of my men."

Disappointment takes over my face, dread grabbing at my stomach as I follow him out of the flaps. "What?"

He lifts a hand to my shoulder, as if willing me to agree with his plan of action. "I must survey home for myself and check on our people."

I fumble, looking around aimlessly. "Papa—I do not understand. You just got back." Firmly, my gaze snaps back to his. I jab a thumb towards the tent, motioning inside. "Liam just scouted out town. And we should be focusing on rescuing Michael."

He interjects with a vigorous head shake. "I thought you shared my concern for our townspeople?"

"I do, Papa, I do." I withhold a sigh, frustrated inside. "But what of Michael? We cannot just leave him to die."

"And we won't." Papa stops abruptly, looking to the ground as his brow furrows in. Pain settles into the lines in his forehead and around his mouth. He looks back up, and I know he's fighting a war inside as he shakes his head. "I have no lead on my son. I have no way of discovering his whereabouts. But I cannot sit idly by while we send out scouts searching for the Dragoon camp. I will pray day and night that the Lord leads me to him. That is our only hope."

The unwavering faith in our God shown on my Papa's face actually fuels the faith in me, the little that is there. He softens his gaze and blinks tired eyes. "I want him back as much as you. And he *will* be back. Right here, right with us." My father's eyes flood, watery at the brim, and I bite my lip till blood penetrates my taste buds to keep from releasing my own floodgates. I force myself to look away as he speaks. "But until I have something that leads us to him, I need to focus on what else is important to us. Our family back home. Do you understand that?"

The way he says family, referring to our friends in River Springs, sends a tiny ripple of warmth through my body, and I find the strength to look up and smile.

"Yes, Sir." I exhale, my breath coming out unsteady. "Just promise me, Papa, that you'll do all you can to come back safely." I search his eyes with mine widened, searching for any sign of reassurance, a promise of return. Biting my cracked lip, I glance around once more. "Papa..."

My voice chokes, a lump forming like it always does before tears stain my cheeks. "I don't want to lose you. I can't. I can't lose you and Michael both." My head finds his burly chest like it's done so many times before.

His arms wrap around me, where I wish they could stay and never leave. "We haven't lost Michael, and you're not going to lose me, sweet one. This is not a dangerous mission—"

"No such thing." I shake my head against his chest. "And I can't help but wonder if they took Michael to lure you in. You heard Liam say that you might be their real target, so what if you're walking into a trap?" I squeeze him tighter.

He releases a chuckle that relaxes my nerves. "When did you become such a strategist? You've learned well. But this isn't as dangerous as you might think. We're only going to scout. We will not engage. The real mission will come soon enough." He sighs, voice quieter. "I just need to see for myself." I nod, squeezing my eyes shut and holding tight. He releases me as an indication that it's time to go, and flashes of memories strike my mind like a lightning bolt, constricting my throat.

I'm twelve years old again, watching him leave our cabin door at the start of the war. Hot tears roll, and panic grips my insides so that I stumble to our doorway. Clutching my stomach, I try to squeeze away the dread inside it, wishing in vain that he'd come back. Those days are over, and yet they seem to be unfolding right before my eyes, and I'm telling him goodbye once again. As he turns, adjusting the tricorne hat on his head, my fingers react in the only way they remember how to, gripping at my stomach as I beg the fear to leave. I bite my lip before a small cry can come out. The words I always wanted to say as he was riding away lie on my tongue.

Come back. Come back.

My mouth opens, ready to release them. But . . .

What would it do? He can't come back. He must leave. It is his duty. I swipe a hand under my eyes and sniff, raising my voice. "Papa!" He turns as I take a step forward, almost into his arms. Searching for something more to say, to keep him here just a little longer. "Will you find out what's of Miss Annie and Lydia?"

The question makes him stumble, I can tell, and for a moment I'm curious as to why. Something takes over his blue eyes that I've never seen before, and his chin tilts up. "As the Lord lives, I will not leave this earth until I see that they are safe."

I hold my breath, jaw slack. Papa rarely swears on the Lord, as he would never dare to falsely. Not near as confident as Papa, I nod hesitantly and smile barely, watching him go.

15

Caretaker

A FIRE GLOWS OUTSIDE the darkened tent. My head tilts to see through the open tent flaps, studying the flames. They brighten the ground with subtle orange flickers. They're pleasant to look at, and I don't mind them occupying my mind.

Beside me, Liam's breathing is deep and full, the fever lowered considerably. All the Lord's work, as a wet rag couldn't be enough to do anything helpful. He stirs, shifting on his side. Fully turned, he stills, facing me.

I've grown comfortable with his silent presence as the day has gone on, but still slightly uneasy with being so near to him while he is unaware. Eventually I'll have to retire to my own tent for the night, but I do wish I could see those piercing green eyes just once and know that he is okay.

As darkness descends outside, I enjoy watching God paint the horizon with deep reds. Watching the growing flames in the sky keeps my mind from other things. Like Papa arriving, only to leave a day later, and Michael not safe by my side. Funny how a fire so small can occupy one's thoughts, but fires have always had that effect on me. My eyelids grow heavy, and I conceal a yawn within my dress's sleeve, tempted to curl up on the ground.

I raise my arms above my head and lace my fingers, pulling towards the sky till I feel a stretch.

A croaky voice stirs at my side. "Maddie?"

My arms fall and I look to my left, behind my shoulder. Liam's eyes shine with their usual green sheen, the color of emerald, though they regard me with something new. Something more intense that makes me scoot back the slightest bit and tuck my hair behind my ear. "Liam . . ." I gulp away my nervousness. "I didn't know you were awake."

"Sorry." The flash in his eyes disappears and his gaze is casual again. "I didn't mean to startle you."

I shake my head. "It's fine. You look much better." Embarrassed that I might be showing too much relief, I deflect my concern. "Papa will be glad to know, he was very concerned about his main messenger." I smile as I fold my legs together on the floor. "How are you feeling?"

"Well." He seems to wince through a faint smile. "I guess I can thank you for that?"

I curse the redness flowing through my cheeks, shrugging to hide it. "I did nothing. It was the Lord who made you well. But you're not out of the woods yet."

I fumble with the dampened rag on the ground, looking downwards. "I expect you to be completely well by morning. I think eight hours of sleep tonight is just what you need."

He nods, suddenly trying to rise with his palms pressed into the blanket.

"Here, let me help you." I reach out, grabbing hold of his shoulders and lifting as hard as I can, though it's no use in trying to hoist up his body weight.

He positions himself, waist bent, hunched over his knees. I raise a brow and watch him, wanting to tell him to lie back down to get the rest he needs. But something tells me he would be too stubborn to listen to anything I say.

I toss the rag to the side, rising and heading for the pitcher of water instead, and I sense Liam's gaze follow me across the grass. Grabbing the pitcher, a lump rises in my throat as I watch my footing, lowering back to the ground by the blanket. The pitcher lands on the ground with a light thud, and I look up to him. He was already watching me, I notice, as my eyes catch his.

My lips stretch into a half smile as I dip the rag into the pitcher. "What?" My voice is shy and alarmingly playful, which I scold myself for after speaking just one word.

Maybe I shouldn't speak at all.

His shoulders rise and fall as he laughs, eyes turning again into green pools. "Nothing."

I almost give a one word reply back, but decide against it, perhaps because nothing comes to mind.

I become suddenly aware that I need to be smart when with Liam O'Dally. I can practically feel my guard falling in his presence, like every wall around my heart is crumbling. He just makes everything so casual and carefree.

I hesitate to look back up, handling the rag, wringing it out twice. It drips heavily, directly onto my dress, and I freeze as I glance up to see the look in his eyes. They burn, searching the deepest part of my heart, as if he knows what lies there.

My breathing quickens as he studies my face. Watching him watch me, I feel myself leaning backwards. Nose twitching and brow furrowing desperately, I suddenly rise with a fast bounce and curl my hands into fists at my side.

"I have to go."

He lifts to a full sitting position. "Go? Where?" His chuckle almost makes me stay, but I step backwards.

"Uh, to find you more food. You're out of chicken." I eye the slice of chicken in the white cloth to the side, gritting my teeth.

Why didn't you say cheese!

Liam finds the chicken, looking back to me with big, handsome, bewildered eyes. He shakes his head abruptly, lifting a pleading brow as if begging me to explain.

I offer an apologetic smile, backing into the tents wall. I flail my hands out pathetically, finding the flaps and spinning, emerging from the tent where I felt I would suffocate from some strange desire.

I groan, holding my stomach and whipping my head to both sides. Food. I need food. That will surely satisfy this confusion. All these new emotions make me yearn not for my Papa, but my Mama. She was my age when she met Papa. But we're at war, and this is no time for romance or even thoughts of love. She would know what to say and tell me what to do. She would pray with me and tell me I'm perfectly normal and these feelings will disappear by morning after I shoot a musket, stomp in some mud, and join in a game of Farkle if the soldiers would allow me.

Perhaps I should take my mother's unsaid advice.

I glance around, walking forwards and then to the side, searching for a game going on, but finding only a couple of crowded groups with five or six soldiers that probably don't want any interruptions. Most are already heading off to bed. My curiosity leads me through the camp, taking me to other tents and fires with meat cooking.

Walking along the dirt path, I let out a long breath of relief.

I knew the confusions would leave if I removed myself from that tent for just a moment. If avoiding him will rid me of these feelings that I wish to have to nothing to do with, then that's exactly what I'll do.

But I promised him food . . .

Well, I sort of did. He did in fact already have chicken.

I stop in the dirt, sighing. My fists clench at my side as my body tenses. I turn and search by one large bonfire, despite the itch to turn away, forget the food, and never enter his tent again.

Several pieces of meat sit in a cloth, untouched by the fire. I snatch them up after finding no solider there to claim them and lengthen my strides. Holding the ends of my dress up in fistfuls and approaching the tent, I swing the flaps open, finding him sitting up. He looks over, locking big eyes on mine as I enter.

"Here." I hand over the chicken without sitting down.

He searches my eyes, slowly taking the sack of meat with the cock of his head. I hold my breath, stepping backwards. My fingers still curl around the ends of my dress.

"Thank you." He barely smiles, almost tentative, and leans on his knees with both forearms.

I nod, swallowing. My hands find the flaps as I slide out, separated from him by letting the flaps fall back in place. Walking away, I pass the glances of soldiers and the faint glows of fires and let my hands fall. A voice in my head says to go back and ask if he needs anything more, or even just company . . .

But the desire to flee from my confusing feelings keeps my feet in the ground, making them move through dirt and take me back to my tent where I curl in a ball up on a wool blanket.

16

A Hound Named Truelove

I TOSS THE BLANKET off my warm body and squeeze away the sleep in the corners of my eyes. I hear birds chirping outside the tent and suddenly realize I've forgotten where I am.

Papa's tent.

Except he is gone, at River Springs, on a mission, and I'm here alone.

Not entirely.

I rise eagerly, stretching my arms above my head. Yes, not entirely alone.

I grab hold of the pitcher and duck under the tent flaps. Warm wind blows my hair out of my face, and I glance upwards. It must be mid-morning already, as the sun is already well into the sky. I tossed and turned without sleeping hardly an hour, yet I'm embarrassed that it will look as if I've lazily slept so late. Hoping no one has noticed, I walk around the tent and approach the side, suddenly catching the suspicious glare of a shaggy soldier. I wrinkle my brow, wary of his near presence. He looks from me to the tent, raising both brows, and makes a mocking snoring sound as heat flows to my cheeks.

I resist rolling my eyes, determined to still be graceful in the midst of strangers. Like my mother. I distract myself with the pitcher, raising a handful of water to my face and rubbing at my puffy eyes. Swooshing a bit in my mouth, I let the rest fall on my hair, washing away several days worth of oil. It soaks my dress, but I don't mind in the sun's heat.

It's been almost twenty-four hours since Papa left and I'm becoming restless, waiting for his return, for news of Michael and of River Springs. The only company in camp is Liam, but how can I be around him when half of me wants to avoid him?

I look to the side, bending to tie my shoes as another breeze sweeps my hair off my shoulders. Anger occasionally boils in my veins, anger at myself, when continual thoughts return to him. Why is it so hard to take thoughts captive, as the Bible commands?

Liam hasn't even emerged from his tent yet this morning. Hopefully a full night of rest after sleeping most of yesterday will allow him to fully recover.

Rising, I walk through the camp that is oddly quiet. Men are comfortable, though some anxious with a desire to fight. They haven't seen battle in awhile. But this is Papa's hidden camp, designed for staying still and not being known, ready to strike wherever needed.

We will stay here as long as he permits it.

The fire closest to my tent has diminished, only a lump of burning coals and ashes. My fingers run along the sides of my dress as I listen to conversations floating through camp, observing games played with wooden dice. A small dog sits at a stool by its owner, eyeing a piece of meat.

I smile, thinking it wouldn't be bad to have a dog as a friend during the war. Without considering it, I walk up to the soldier, looking down at the hound. The dog's ears perk and it rises to its hind legs, then lowers to my feet. "Is she yours?"

The soldier peers up, his dark eyes warming upon seeing me, and tilts his head. "Ma'am. No, Truelove's not my own." He eyes the dog with a conflicted glare.

I smile back, bending to the dog and letting my small sack of food bounce in my hand. She approaches with young brashness, fumbling with the meat. The soldier sighs, leaning on his leg with both folded hands. "She wondered into camp about the same time as your father the other evening. Since he was coming back from the north, I jokingly named her Truelove, after General Washington's favorite dog."

I snap both eyes up, jaw dropping. "You're kidding? I've read stories about the general and his dogs." Looking back down, I study the dog I suddenly recognize as English. A hound, without a doubt. Washington has foxhounds he uses for hunting and companionship. Everyone knows he adores the canines, his favorites being Sweet Lips, Venus, and . . .

"Truelove!" I say the pup's name with a smile, her head cocking. I tilt my head, lifting the hounds face to my eyes in wonder. "You're a runaway pup, hmm?" The dog pants, pressing it's face into my hand to chew the skin. Shaking my head, I look up to the soldier who I originally thought was the owner. This dog doesn't belong to any soldier. It just might belong to the dearly loved George Washington himself!

The dog finishes the scraps in my hand and I rise, folding my arms. "What will we do to return her?"

The soldier glances down, hesitant, and scratches the side of his beard with short fingers. "Ma'am, I don't mean to throw this on you, but . . . Truelove needs someone to care for her and," he looks up, pursing his lips with great consideration, "no soldier's gonna want to watch her." He looks behind his back, as if considering an option too risky to say aloud. He lowers to a whisper, leaning in. "Could you care for her till she is returned to her master?"

I open my mouth with widened eyes.

Of course, I would love to care for the pup, but a part of me wants to focus on nothing else but Michael. Then again, what can I do for him while here alone?

"I can do that." I smile, nodding from him to the hound.

"Thank you, Miss, thank you." The solider seems tired, perhaps from trying to find a rescue for this pup. I nod farewell, the small pooch wagging its tail while falling in step with my fast strides. It playfully barks at my dress's swaying ends as I laugh, walking between tents until we arrive at a fire with food, knowing Liam will be hungry upon waking. Eventually I find pieces of beef, a container with some kind of stew sitting by an unattended, small fire.

I glance about, grabbing the food that no soldier seems to want. Walking to the tent, the flaps sway slightly from a soft breeze. I swing them back, stepping through.

Liam looks up, brows raised as he buttons up the white cotton shirt hanging past his waist.

"Oh—" I stop, catching his glance, gripping the food in my hands. "I didn't realize you were awake."

His blonde hair sticks to his face in strands and the fire in his green eyes is back. He tucks in his shirt with one hand. "I just woke up. What's been happening in camp while I've been missing in action?"

Moving to the wooden stand in the corner of the tent, I set down the sack of meat and can of stew. "Nothing interesting. Just soldiers playing games and making fires. I found a dog. George Washington's hound, actually." I let a teasing smirk tug my lips, returning in front of him and tilting my head.

A curious smile tilts the corners of his mouth up. "What?"

"Well—" I shake my head, "I didn't actually find her. A soldier did, but I'm taking care of her for him until we can return her to Washington. How are you feeling?"

He looks down at me through a winsome gaze, sidestepping me and pushing back the tent's flaps. "Great. As if nothing happened at all." I nod even though he's already past me and calm my beating heart, turning to follow. "How could Washington's dog have gotten lost?" He looks against the sun, observing the soldiers. "I don't get it."

I come up beside him outside the tent, raising a hand above my eyes to block the sun's glare. "I've been wondering the same thing. Maybe you can help me return her after we rescue Michael and things return to normal."

I hear him pause, shifting slightly towards me. "Normal? I'm not sure what that will look like after the war." He seems to think for a moment, careful to reply, and when he looks at me, his eyes tell me it all. "At some point, I need to get back home. My Momma's still there and needs two hands to keep a roof over her head. Little Natalie still needs her big brother." It's the first time he's mentioned his sister. A smirk tugs his lips, but I see the longing in his eyes. He wants home, he needs his family, and the hard truth reveals itself before my eyes like a dark curtain whipping back.

Liam O'Dally won't stick around for long after the colonel releases him.

How could I have expected anything else? A part of me should be relieved. So why do I hurt? Why does it sting?

"She likes you." Liam looks to Truelove now, raising a brow. He licks his lips, whistling to the hound who comes up to his legs and walks through them as he takes a step after another. Her playful bark sends a laugh bubbling in my throat and a chuckle rippling through Liam's chest. I squeeze my side, biting down hard on my bottom lip and watching his eyes follow Truelove's tail that wags vigorously from side to side.

A loud commotion startles us both.

We look at each other, both moving quickly without saying a word. I lift my eyes above the bobbing heads ahead and rush into the sea of men, feeling Liam close behind. Hair stands on the back of my neck at the possibilities.

Could it be Papa? Has he rescued Michael?

No, that would be too soon, but what if God answered our prayers?

I fling my hair off my shoulders, using all the strength I have to push past wide and narrow shoulder alike, all much bigger than mine.

Then my eyes catch it. The brown eyes of a quarter horse, its mane milky white.

"Faithful?" I become more curious than excited, confused as to why she would be here. Her white head jerks up and down, revealing its rider's countenance every few seconds, and then I understand. The horse's head shoved downwards, my entire face lights, and I move from Liam and deeper into the crowds to reach my Papa. A laugh bubbles over and out loud. Joyfully. Barely do I feel a hint of strength rise as the joy increases, and I welcome it fully.

Finally making it past the group, I dive past the final few men and in front of Faithful, swinging both arms around her neck. A leg swings over the saddle and I bounce up in the air and back down, ready to hug him. But as he lands, another set of legs, draped in long, pretty cloth, swings over the saddle with the help of my Papa's arms.

My jaw drops, feelings of relief and excitement and confusion slamming into me front on. I raise my hands to my face, squeal in delight, and rush into a pair of arms other than my Papa's.

"Miss Annie!!" Her rosy locks drape over my shoulders as I hold as tight as I can, lifting my eyes above the saddle and shrieking in shock. Little Lydia bounces on the saddle, urgent to get down at this moment, her golden curls blowing in the wind. I look from Miss Annie to her daughter, shaking my head, fumbling for words. "How did this—I mean—you both are safe! I can't believe—" I stop short, looking this time to Papa, running fingers through Faithful's mane. "How did you ever do it, Papa?"

He grins the widest grin I've seen on him since years have passed and shrugs both wide shoulders. "I told you, as the Lord lives, I would see to it that they were safe. By His grace, I kept my promise."

I press my lips together in wonderful bewilderment, hugging Miss Annie again and again in excitement at what this means. Not only are the two girls I love dearly safe, but staying at camp will not be dreadful any longer. Having other females as company makes me excited for the days ahead.

I gesture to both of them after Lydia is securely on the ground and holding onto her Mama's hand. "I will show you our tent and we will talk for hours, and Lydia! I must show you Truelove!" I stop to catch my breath like I always do when hurrying to speak my mind before I forget what there is to say, and then I turn to Papa at the mention of the hound. "Oh, Papa. Something terrible and equally wonderful has happened. I've found General Washington's lost pup, Truelove. We must return her—"

His eyes glance back and forth from both of mine and I know immediately he isn't convinced. "Excuse me? Where did you find a dog?"

My brow furrows. "Well, I can't be sure it's his, but it's like the ones he owns, and it responds to the name as if it is correct." I practice patience in my voice and posture, explaining the story as Lydia listens with round eyes. "And I can't imagine the torment dear Washington must be feeling without knowing where she's gone off to."

Papa wrinkles his nose like I've done myself many times, a bit disturbed. "Never heard of a grown man, especially that of a general, with so much love for his dogs."

I jerk my head back in defense, as if it's my duty to defend Washington. "It is perfectly normal for a man to cherish his pets."

"It's a bit odd."

I look over, surprised to see it was Liam who made the comment. My mouth drops as I refrain from showing annoyance at their prejudice. "It is not! Are the two of you daring to discourage your own general of adoring his dogs, then?" I lift a brow in both their directions.

They simultaneously raise both hands in innocence, pulling their heads back. "No Ma'am." Papa's smile is clearly seen by the low sunlight as mid-day begins to settle around us in cooler colors, the sky now a dark blue.

"Not I." Liam's eyes sparkle towards mine.

I tilt my chin jokingly, bending to grip Lydia's hand. "Good. Now that that's settled, let's get you both to a tent." Gripping Faithful's reins, I nod to the girls who look winded and tired from the long journey to a camp they know nothing about. I catch Liam throw an unsure glance at Papa about Truelove, which I choose to ignore.

"You ladies will stay with Maddie in my tent and I'll move over to Brenley's," Papa says, ever the gentleman.

A smile slides upon my mouth as I pull up alongside Miss Annie and take her hand. "I can't believe you both are here. You will have to tell me everything."

She blinks brown, tired eyes, and her smile is small though still just as kind. "Dear, our home is not the same anymore." She lifts a hand to my shoulder as we walk. A soldier jogs up to my side and offers to take Faithful's reins. I smile and slide them into his palm. "You wouldn't recognize it." Miss Annie's voice is sweet and smooth, calming my nerves that have worked up since this morning even though her words are grave. Miss Annie has always had this effect on people, able to bring peace to those present no matter what her words are. I slip my arm through hers, listening as we scan our boots shuffling through grass. "So much is destroyed, so much . . . gone. I want to believe we can rebuild, but with most of the men either off at war or their lives having now been taken by those awful Dragoons . . ." I see her lift all fingertips to her lips, concealing a tremble. Her eyes are wide and wet as she looks at me. "I just don't know, Maddie. I can only pray the Lord redeems what was lost."

My eyes soften with compassion as I stop to face her fully, my voice hardly strong. "It won't always be like this. We have to believe that." I hope my face does not show my own doubt in the words I haven't even come to believe myself. Still, I offer Miss Annie a sorrowful smile as she nods quietly, and we walk into the tent arm in arm.

Papa carries Lydia inside while speaking over his shoulder to Liam. "Gather the officers for an update and strategy meeting."

"Sir." Liam hurries away to prepare the meeting.

Papa nods to the rest of us as he sets Lydia down and walks up to me, straight and tall. I watch him with steady eyes, noticing the mysterious smile that lies on his lips.

"I found him."

17
FEATHERS OF HIS WINGS

HIS WORDS MAKE ME GASP as my stomach drops. Not able to conceal a grin, I throw my arms around his waist. "Where Papa? Where is he?"

He inhales sharply, placing a hand to my arm as if to prepare me for the news. "A Dragoon camp—less than a day's ride from here. It's all I know, but I've been told that Kel and Tomah have found details." He smiles brightly, nodding. "They arrived just before I did. They'll brief us so we can plan a rescue."

Hardly able to gather my thoughts, hearing him mention a rescue, my eagerness overtakes me and I quicken. "Please, Papa, let me come to the meeting.

He watches me for a moment, silent, then slides out of my grip and motions to the girls. "You should stay with our new guests, Maddie. You will learn of everything soon."

"I'll stay with Lydia," Miss Annie interjects. She shakes her head firmly. "We won't step outside the tent until you return. Maddie should be with you."

Papa watches her and folds both arms against his chest, fingering his coat's material. "Alright. Maddie, come with me."

I feel my eyes widen. Trying to contain my excitement, I come up behind him as he exits the tent. Smiling back gratefully to Miss Annie before stepping out, I soon emerge back into the chaos of camp. It takes every ounce of restraint within me to not ask questions just yet. Papa's strides are terribly long, making me strain to keep up with him. Thankfully the headquarters tent is not far, and men are already gathered under the large canvas waiting for Papa to begin the briefing.

Upon entering, Papa nods to Brenley.

Brenley's face brightens with a grin of relief. "Sir! We were just about to get the report from Kel. Thank the Lord you made it back from River Springs without encountering those Dragoons."

Papa starts without a moment to waste. "I've confirmed for myself that River Springs is in a grave state. But we have hope." He points a finger to the tent's ceiling and nods firmly. "I understand the Lord blessed us this day with information on where the Dragoons are camped and confirmation that Michael is okay." He turns to one of his most trusted soldiers. "Kel, let's hear what you've got. I'm guessing the Lord used Tomah's gift for tracking to help get this information?" He looks to the Indian. I had not even noticed that Tomah was in the headquarters tent, filthy from a full day and two entire nights of tracking and probably little to no sleep, but grinning from ear to ear due to the success of his efforts. I'd rarely ever seen an Indian up close until this adventure started a few days ago, and now I've seen him smile in a way that makes him seem like one of the family.

Kel steps up to the table, pointing at the map as he speaks. As the youngest soldier of the elite four that Papa has personally walked alongside, his eyes are still young and bright as he leans on the table with folded fists against his chin. "We started following Peterson two nights ago. Fields, Tomah, and myself. He had a few hours ahead of us and was smart enough to leave fake trails headed the wrong way in several places. But

Tomah figured it out and we discovered the Dragoon camp by noon yesterday. We waited until nightfall to get a closer look."

Kel raises thick eyebrows Papa's way, showing a smirk. "That patience paid off in a big way. Fields is still back there watching their movements with the understanding that he is to race here immediately to signal if the Dragoons break camp."

I can't stop from interrupting. "But what about Michael? Did you see him?"

Kel smiles, looking at me with gentle eyes. "Yes. Fields can sneak up on anyone or anything and he managed to get close enough to both hear their plans and confirm that Michael is still okay. But there was no way for us to get him out without more men to cause a distraction. We need at least three more men for an effective extraction."

Relief floods over our small group at the mention of Michael being alive and well. All seemed relieved except Papa, who is intent on getting every detail possible. "Plans? What plans did you hear them discuss?" Papa holds his hand in the air in question, eyeing Kel. "Tell me everything Fields learned."

Kel hesitates only for a second, looking at the map then straight into Papa's eyes. He seems to pause as he considers the right words. "They want you, Sir. Something about orders to use whatever means necessary to capture you alive."

Liam speaks up, seeming fully recovered with an intensity of purpose in his voice once again. "Yes, we heard as much from witnesses at River Springs." He turns to Kel, curious, and lifts a hand to the nape of his neck frustratingly. "Why? Were you able to discover anything about their reasons?"

Kel's look of bewilderment does not help, but his words reveal more than anyone in the room except Papa and me could know. "They kept talking about some general. Akers?" I fumble with my dress as he struggles. "No, Ashton, that was it. General Ashton."

At the sound of the revengeful name of the general, my Papa's eyes flash with contempt. I only know half of the story between the two men, but it goes all the way back to when my mother was alive, as her beauty was the main cause of their feud.

Quickly, Papa changes the subject, looking down for only a moment. "What about Peterson? Were you able to confirm how much information that spy able to give them?"

Kel does not miss a beat. "Thick as thieves, he's definitely one of them. But if Grover is in on it, then Peterson had no idea because he was laughing to the other Dragoons that Grover was foolish enough to send him out, which made the perfect escape."

Brenley shakes his head side to side. "Grover's definitely not a spy. I'm convinced he only sent Peterson because he knew the colonel wanted Liam to be the one watching over Miss Holt." I bite my lip. My eyes flicker over to Liam and I hope Papa doesn't notice. Liam stares hard at the dirt ground in thought, arms folded.

Papa has been deep in thought since the mention of General Ashton. Perhaps he's trying to figure out why the general would let their personal animosity consume such a valuable tool of the British as their Dragoons. The mention of Peterson being with the Dragoons snaps him back to the conversation as he glances up, brows raised. "That means they know the location of our camp, the number of our forces, even our routine. This regiment is in grave danger."

Kel is nodding quickly, as if reading Papa's mind. "And that's exactly what they were arguing about in the Dragoon camp. Whether to attack our camp and take you by force or send a message to lure you in. They believe we are fairly evenly matched and some did not want to risk a frontal assault."

Brenley is suddenly excited. "Well now, it appears the tables have turned and we are the ones with the information and the advantage. I say we break camp immediately and attack their camp before they reach a decision!"

"No!" Papa's voice seems to shake the tent's walls. He pauses, flexing his jaw. "Michael would never survive the attack. First, we initiate a stealth rescue . . . tonight."

His eyes dart from side to side furiously, an image of rescue forming in his mind. His voice peaks with vigor. "That's the only chance to save Michael. It has to be a small group to avoid detection. Get in, get Michael, and get out without being seen. Once Michael is safe, then we can attack if circumstances are right. Kel, I trust your judgment." He turns to the solider. "You think six of our best is the perfect number?"

Kel nods confidently. "I do, Sir. We have an excellent lay of the land, we watched their movements for a full day and night, so we know when they change overwatch. We already mapped out their weaknesses."

Liam moves beside Kel, pointing to them both, then Tomah and Woods. "Sir, you've trained us for exactly this type of mission. We know what to do. We'll get Michael back to you."

"How far to the Dragoon camp?"

Kel clears his throat. "Two hours by horseback, but I'd suggest the last three miles by foot to avoid detection." He looks back to Liam with raised brows. "They have spotters stationed two miles out from camp. That will add at least another two hours even at a steady pace."

Papa nods in agreement. "Then we leave as soon as possible. Your squad of four plus me. We'll meet Fields there."

Liam turns to his men while everyone turns to the map. "Tomah, you're going to take out two of those sentries one at time, using your blade. That will clear our path and provide Kel and myself with Dragoon uniforms to get into camp. We'll be right behind you, so simply make your move and drop the Dragoons. We'll get the uniforms once you've taken out the second one, then you move close enough to the camp to keep an eye on the tent where they are holding Michael." Liam points to a clump of trees outside the two-mile scout perimeter of the camp. "Go." He motions to Tomah with the raise of his hand. "Relay the plan to Fields and meet us here." Tomah leaves without saying a word or even nodding.

I shudder at the thought of Liam waltzing right into that den of evil. But before I can think too much about it, he has moved to the next man on the team, and I'm captured by the way he takes command with respect and leadership. I'm captured by the way he moves when he talks. Confident, yet humble. "Woods, you're our best at distance. Find high ground and be prepared to take out anyone blocking our path out of camp once we have Michael."

I notice a sly grin creeping up on Woods face, but it erases just as quickly with a serious nod. Kel points to a place on the map. "There, Woods. It's a perfect place for overwatch. You'll be able to see their entire camp and see us coming in from the southeast here." He sweeps across from the ridge chosen for Woods to the place where he and Liam will enter the camp dressed as Dragoons.

Kel turns to Liam. "Lieutenant, they change posts at three a.m. That's when we have to make our move. Fields will be able to direct us to Michael's tent."

Papa has watched them make their plans and listens intently, trying to defer to his men for the plan. "I should be with you to get Michael so that he knows it's us, knows we're friendly. He will not recognize either of you."

Kel thinks intently for a long moment. "I don't think so, Sir. You'd be recognized as an officer, definitely not a sentry since you are so much, um, well—"

"Older?" Papa let's a smile loose.

Kel releases a sigh, fumbling as Liam rescues him. "Colonel, you're the one they want." His brow tightens. "We should not have you marching into the middle of their camp when we will be so outnumbered. You said it best earlier. In and out, without being discovered. That's our best chance. And I really like the idea of knowing you are out there with Woods and watching the whole thing, able to send him wherever is needed during the mission."

Papa looks at Liam, doubtful. "I appreciate the thought. I'll keep my distance unless it's absolutely necessary to intervene—"

"Wait, wait, I know how you can let Michael know you're with us." My mouth gets ahead of my head as I interrupt the exchange, causing Papa to look at me with disapproving eyes. I fumble with my dress and reach for the treasure in my pocket that I've carried with me every minute of the last three days to remind me to pray for Michael constantly.

"He'll recognize this." I hold up the wooden soldier, Uncle Henry's fine work. "He saw it the day of the attack when I tried to give it to him, but Sarah . . ." I shake my head, tensing. "Never mind that, the point is he'll know it's from me." I shove the piece towards Liam. "Take it, take it. I promise it will work."

He reaches for it, letting it fall in his hands as a pair of rich eyes send a ripple of warmth through me. "I'll take good care of it." His tone is confident, much more than my own as I thank him. He smiles, slipping the wooden soldier in his bag.

All of the men turn to the maps on the table to run through the mission once more before moving out. Maps cover the table as they scatter among ink pens and blank paper. Meanwhile, I try to figure out where I fit into all these plans. Sensing a pause in the discussion, I gently try to get his attention.

"Papa?"

No response.

"Papa?" I say louder, squeezing between him and Liam. "What can I do? I should be there when Michael is rescued."

"You will be, Maddie. You'll be at our home in River Springs waiting for us. We'll be there by sunrise. I'm sending William and Simpson with you. I need you to check on the people back home, see what you can do to help Dr. Rush. He needs you more than we do right now."

Help the Doctor? He wants me to wash rags and stitch wounds instead of helping with the rescue?

"But Papa—"

"No, Maddie. There is no time, and that Dragoon camp is no place for you. Please just do as I say. Michael's life could depend up on it."

My protest is useless. His mind is made and he's probably right. My sneaking out from Sarah is hardly proper training for the stealth needed on this mission.

"Yes, Papa."

"Good." His eyes say more than his words, as if he understands my yearning. He nods, as if to say there will be another day, a different time for me to do my part. Yet I yearn all the more to do my part now . . . whatever that is. Will I ever know?

Papa turns to Brenley. "Start organizing a break of camp and move the entire regiment just outside River Springs. It will take you a full day's march to get there. It is nearing noon. Leave within the hour and march through the night. If the Dragoons change their mind and move for a surprise attack tonight, you'll already be gone in the opposite direction. Hopefully they stay put and we can extract Michael by morning's light, then meet you in River Springs." Papa looks across the eager faces of the men, each of them ready for action. "Any questions?"

"Sir, if I may." Liam seems to not want to question a decision of the colonel.

"Speak, lieutenant, but make it quick."

"Are you sure River Springs is a safe place for your family?"

Realization dawns on Papa's face even as Liam is finishing his thoughts. "Once we rescue Michael, why would the Dragoons not just head straight to River Springs and attack again? We are evenly matched, but all of those citizens and especially your family will be caught right in the middle if there is a battle."

Brenley nods, rejoining the conversation. "Safe Haven, John, we need a safe haven for your family and the people of River Springs. Remember that valley southeast of Green Mountain, where we camped after Fort Dobbs was attacked by the Cherokee?"

Papa's face lights up with recognition as Brenley's suggestion weaves perfectly into his plan.

"Yes, it's ideal for food and water, as well as security with the ridges on all sides where we can place spotters! We'll evacuate River Springs, take the regiment there until I can report to Continental Headquarters and determine the next course of action." Papa grins, pleased. "Excellent idea Brenley, I'm counting on you to lead the regiment there immediately and set up the new camp, securing the area. As discussed, still have William and Simpson take Maddie directly to River Springs. She can tell the people of our plan and by the time we get there at sunrise, they should be ready to move out for the new location." His settled mind casts his confident gaze from Brenley to Liam and then settles on me, full of hope.

Brenley and his men are quickly in motion and out of the tent.

Liam turns to Kel and Woods. "Get the horses ready, enough food and water for twenty-four hours. Pass the orders to William and Simpson. They are to take Maddie to River Springs tonight and we'll meet them there in the morning."

They nod and immediately are on the move.

Papa stops them, calling after. "Kel, also have William and Simpson break down your tents and mine, bringing only the light essentials to meet us in River Springs tomorrow. We'll have at least one night of camp between there and the safe haven. Send the rest of my things with the regiment."

Liam is turning to leave but quickly stops, turning back to me and placing a hand on my shoulder. "I'm bringing Michael back to you, Maddie. I'm going to make this right." Before I can respond, I barely catch the flash of his green eyes and he's out of the tent, leaving Papa and myself in the tent alone.

Papa, looking even more serious than before, looks at the entrance of the tent to make sure everyone is gone. He turns his full attention on me. "Maddie, I don't know what will happen tonight. I don't know why after all these years Ashton would still want revenge. But if we fail to rescue Michael tonight, if they capture me..."

I squeeze my eyes shut. "No, Papa, I can't even imagine—"

"Hush now. I do not believe that will happen. Liam and his men were chosen for this regiment because of their skill and I've trained them personally. I believe we'll get Michael and be in River Springs by morning." Papa looks behind my shoulder, lowering his voice as his eyes pierce mine. "But there is always a risk and you must know what to do next if I don't arrive."

I stumble a bit, trying not to acknowledge the possibility while also trying to show him I can handle this. "I—I understand. I do. And I can obey orders." Firmly, my gaze snaps back to his.

"You have to get back to the regiment and arrive at the new safe haven."

I tighten my brow, conflicted. "But how would I find them? Does William or Simpson know the location?"

"*You* know it." Papa takes my shoulders. "Remember the Turtle Rock? The one so high it took us all day to climb?"

I feel a smile, nodding. "Of course, Papa."

"Get there. Once on top, you'll be able to see the regiment's new location and find your way to them."

"But there won't be a need," I read his eyes, breathing fast, "because you'll get Michael tonight and you'll be in River Springs by sunrise to lead the evacuation, right?"

I don't like what I see behind his eyes. It's not the certainty I was hoping for, but there's at least some sense of hope that Michael will soon be free.

He lifts his gaze up. "I will pray throughout this night as we travel that the Lord prepares our path and guides our steps."

I see and taste the peace that comes over him and fills the tent.

Leaning into his side, I whisper only for him. "I don't want to leave, Papa. I can't leave you." I look up to see compassionate eyes. I know he understands, but I also know he'll do everything in his power to protect me.

His hand strokes my hair. "Little one, do not fret. Have you forgotten so easily that the angels are on your side?"

I look down, ashamed.

How *could* I have forgotten so easily? I barely look up, almost hoping to see a flicker of doubt in his eyes as well, to know I'm at least not the only one. But steadfast hope lies there instead.

How? How are they so strong, while I'm so weak?

Papa, obviously eager for justice, says nothing more, simply kissing my forehead and then turning to walk away swiftly. Watching him disappear, I suddenly realize that it's the first time I am eager to see him go. Excited that he's on his way to rescue Michael.

And I'm somehow at peace, knowing that even on a mission as dangerous as such, his steps are secured by the Almighty, covered by the feathers of His wings.

18

Left Behind

THE ENTIRE CAMP BUZZES with action, a controlled chaos that will have the entire regiment packed and marching in less than an hour. Everyone seems to have something urgent to do.

Everyone, that is, except me.

It feels like one of those days at home when the house was buzzing with action, but all I wanted to do was sneak out to Miss Annie's . . .

Miss Annie!

How could I have forgotten that Annie and Lydia were here? I nearly trip over everything and everyone in sight as I rush to Papa's tent to tell the girls they won't even get one night to rest here in camp.

Peeking through the tent to see the girls chat as mother and daughter, my shoulders fall. I study them in silence, hurting with regret. A wound opens, and I study it briefly. It aches with the sting of my mother's death, not willing to go away for good. I hold back a sniff, clenching my dress and letting the wound close. I move the flap with a hand, entering with excitement to tell the girls of the rescue plans.

Miss Annie looks up, revealing a sparkling grin. "Maddie! Join us, will you?"

"I think I will." I plop down beside them, gathering Lydia onto my lap. "The meeting is over." I raise both brows at Miss Annie in elation. "Plans for Michael are made."

"Oh, Praise God!" She reaches back to swing her hair over one shoulder, starting to braid with a soft smile.

I nod, running fingers through Lydia's tangled curls. "Everyone will be breaking camp immediately. I'm sorry you only just arrived, but you'll be leaving within the hour."

Miss Annie furrows her brow, pausing on the braid to let her hands rest at her bent waist. "Breaking camp? Whatever do you mean?"

"The order was given by Papa. The spy that left camp and traveled to the Dragoon's campground has all the information he needs to organize a raid." I sigh, twisting Lydia's golden hair into a small bun. "We must leave immediately for the new safe haven." I tighten my brow, scrunching my nose. "*I'm* going with William and Simpson back home to help Dr. Rush, though I would much prefer helping rescue Michael."

Miss Annie looks at me from the side, widened eyes unblinking. She slowly looks away, then stands all at once. "Heaven's sake. We must hurry, then. Come, Lydia. Let's see what we can do to help."

I watch Lydia bounce off my lap as I pause, forgetting the matters at hand momentarily. She's so young. Shouldn't have to grow up in this war. She dances and twirls, spins and skips. Giggling in complete oblivion to the danger present and to a melody only she hears. I barely smile, wondering if we would all be better off if we could dance away our troubles alike to one as she, an angel of only five years. The little girl is abandoned to the morning, forgetting the night.

"Gather tents four and five! Six and seven next!" A commanding voice jolts me to the side. I exhale, rising to brush off my dress and push the flaps back. The sun still hangs high in the sky, not yet told by God to start setting. Hopefully Papa and the men will be leaving as soon as it starts to lower and the air starts to cool. I raise a hand to shade my eyes, squinting at the movement ahead. Officers fold the tents, loading them onto a small wagon used for cargo and the like. I step out of the tent, watching them pack tent after tent along with chests and sacks of leftover meat.

"Eight and nine." A soldier nods to his comrade, swinging a sack of beans onto the wagon. He wipes a strand of black hair out of his sweaty face with an arm. I walk tentatively, pursing my lips. Upon approaching, the soldier turns, still loading sack after sack. A gentle smile tugs his lips.

"Sir." I dip my head, raising both eyes to meet his. "Would you happen to know where William and Simpson are?

The soldier, younger than most in camp, pauses his sack-loading, wiping both hands on brown pant legs. "I saw them near the Headquarters tent near half an hour ago." His eyes slightly gleam. "Would you like me to take you there?"

"No," I hurry, "it's alright." I back away, nodding. "Thank you, uh—"

"Maverick." The dark-haired soldier smiles and lifts another sack to load.

The Headquarters tent isn't far, though I can't imagine how I didn't find the men there before. I rush between the tents that have yet to be taken down, ignoring soldiers who hurry around in orderly chaos.

Approaching the tent, I peak through the flaps, raising both brows. "William?"

The dark-skinned soldier looks up from a map spread across the table.

"Ah, yes, Miss Holt?"

I don't bother with stepping in, making the conversation short. "Have you decided what time we will be leaving?"

William sidesteps the table, folding large hands neatly at his waist. "I expect soon. Maybe an hour after the regiment is gone. That will give us time to create some false tracks out of camp to confuse any of the enemy that might come later tonight or tomorrow. Miss Holt, it's going to be a hard ride, but there is time for you to rest a bit while we help pack up the regiment." He pauses with a wide grin, "Though word around camp was that you already slept pretty late today."

Embarrassed, I lift up my chin curtly. "Well, yes, it was a late morning. But I actually I slept very little last night—I believe I will take advantage of the time to rest." I fumble with my dress then let the tent flaps close as I leave.

The sun beats warmly on my back, lowering as dusk begins its descent. Lifting my eyes, I find Miss Annie and Lydia loading up a small, traveling wagon. Walking briskly in their direction, I join in the work and grab a sack of supplies to load.

Flicking my glance to the side, I notice across the camp that Gen. Smeed is clearly arguing with William and Simpson. Perhaps trying to insert his false authority once again. I'm sure I'll get the whole story during our ride to River Springs after the regiment leaves.

Finished loading, Miss Annie and Lydia pile in the wagon and prepare to leave. I kiss them both goodbye, tossing Lydia's curly hair before walking away. "Do our people and your Papa proud now." Miss Annie grins, eyes twinkling.

I tilt my chin up, nodding with affirmation. "I will."

Somehow.

I head back to Papa's tent to make sure things are ready for William and Simpson to break down. Other than Papa's and the four from Liam's squad, every other tent in camp has already been broken down and packed up. Papa's larger items are off in the wagon with Annie and Lydia and all that is left inside the tent is his cot. Even Truelove has gone with the ladies, so the tent feels cold and lonely. I sit down on the cot, going through my pack to make sure I've got everything for the ride to River Springs. I find my pocket Bible quickly, the journal with all of Mama's sayings, a full canteen, my dagger, and the one thing Papa said I should always have when I'm in the woods, especially exploring alone.

A flintlock pistol held tightly in a leather holster, retrieved the first day we arrived in camp. My fingers grip the cool handle, and for the first time I realize that this is what I've trained for. Isn't it? To use the weapon I've been given and let courage rise . . . to fight?

Next is a small sack of food. Chicken, cheese, and bread. I set the pack on the ground and lie back on the cot to think about the night ahead, praying for God's protection over everyone on this very precarious evening. The high energy events of the day have had me on edge for several hours and now, all of the sudden, laying here all alone, my eyelids become heavy. Three nights in a row with very little sleep begins to catch up with me.

It wouldn't hurt to rest for a few minutes . . .

The guys are busy packing up their own things and Liam's tents anyways.

Everything seems to get heavier as I give into the weariness, exhaustion pulling me into a sweet dream of reunion with Michael.

***

I can feel myself smiling in my sleep. I hear crickets all around me, and I slowly realize the reunion with

Michael is just a dream. The rescue mission has not yet occurred.

I wake up to . . .

Nothing.

Complete silence, other than the crickets.

I dart from the cot to the front of the tent's flaps only to find the entire camp empty.

All the tents, except the ones William and Simpson were supposed to get for Papa, Liam and his squad—gone! All the soldiers—gone!

Where are William and Simpson? Surely they would not go on to River Springs without me? Why have they not broken down the tents? Where did I see them last?

Oh no. General Smeed.

They were with the arrogant general before breaking camp.

Surely, he did not once again stick his nose where it does not belong and send them on some errand.

We were supposed to go to River Springs!

Panic settles deep in the pit of my stomach. How could the entire regiment not notice these few tents still here? Even in the chaos, these tents are so obvious that someone should have asked why they were not broken down.

Could they possibly have thought Papa and Liam's squad had simply not left yet? Or perhaps that they're coming back later tonight? Whatever the reason, one thing is for sure.

I am alone.

In the middle of the wilderness.

In the middle of a war.

I have no idea which direction the regiment went, presumably with my missing escorts, William and Simpson.

And then I hear it. It's the obvious sound of my horse, Faithful. I'm not alone after all.

As I walk towards her, I can see in her eyes that she felt alone as well and is just as happy to see me as I am her. Warm affections stir in me for the mare. And then a map flashes in my mind. The map Liam and Papa and the men were pointing to as they planned. I saw everything about their rescue mission. I can see the map now, and I can see the exact path they said they were going to take. I close my eyes, tracing the map. It's my only chance, but I've got to move now if I'm going to get there before the rescue is over and they ride for River Springs. And I will no longer be alone. I'll be surrounded by Dragoons!

So there it is.

My mission has changed. I must get to the outskirts of the Dragoon camp that I saw on the map, and I must get there in time to join up with Papa and his men after they rescue Michael.

Well, Maddie. You wanted to be in the thick of things. You wanted to know what it was like to ride alone in the wilderness like a messenger. Enough thinking about it, it's time to go!

Soon, I'm standing before the world of woods stretching miles along, holding Faithful's reins in my hand, my pack already tied to the back of the saddle. I breathe in, considering my actions.

I must do this.

For Michael. For River Springs.

I step my leather boot into the stirrup hanging down Faithful's side and swing up and over just like I've done a thousand times before.

One last look at the tents being left behind and the black forest ahead of me, with a slight nudge into Faithful's side, we're off into the forest once again.

But this time, I face the endless trees and crevices as a foe, not a friend.

19
FLICKERS A MILE AWAY

THE RAIN STARTED AS a trickle less than an hour into my journey. Now the forest drip and thunder claps above the trees. I hug Faithful even tighter with my legs, the saddle horn in my hands, determined to keep up my speed even with the dangerous ride. So far I've managed to follow the river bank just like the map on the table had said but now, with so much rain, the bank is getting too slick and I'm working my way through higher ground. I constantly look down at the bank and stop far too often to be sure I'm heading the right way.

Papa had taught me to navigate my direction with the stars, but ever since the storm got heavy, the dark skies now hide my normal glittery guides. Squinting through water droplets, I open my mouth, drinking in as much rain water as I can. I filled my canteen earlier when the downpour first started. As the canvas of the forest grows dark and thick, sight of the river dims. I listen for the rushing river above the pounding rain and cracking thunder, but it slowly becomes dim too. I squint my eyes, leaning forward, standing in the slippery stirrups. The mud splashes as Faithful stomps through puddles, bitter cold rain falling onto us both. My eyes drift left and right, and I focus back on the path Papa and his men probably took. Thunder shakes my body, striking in my ears. I look straight ahead, willing the dark to leave and the thunder to subside, shaking wet strands of hair out of my face.

Panic quickly begins to settle in my throat.

I lay forward onto Faithful's neck, stroking and petting her, not sure if I am reassuring her or she is me. I press my thick, sticky hair into my face, anything for warmth, and dare to keep moving forward, even as darkness makes every step of Faithful more treacherous. But like her name, she remains faithful to obey my every command, whether from the nudge of my knee into her side or the slight twist of the reins to the left or right. We move as one and keep forging ahead one hoof at a time.

Am I even going the right way?

With the forest so dark, I've lost my sense of direction, and terror settles deep in my bones, desperate for a breath of bravery. I grunt, Faithful slipping slightly in the mud and almost tumbling before regaining her balance. A sudden crack of lightning illuminates before me two paths, one on the left and one on the right.

Papa and the soldiers could have taken either one.

Frightened by the reality of being completely and utterly lost, I open my mouth to call out Papa's name, but let it close with a whimper. Hot tears burn on my skin in contrast with the cold rain. If I call out, it could give away our position to the British, and therefore, harm Michael. I don't know how close I am to the Dragoon camp and cannot risk it. I've lost track of time, but I know it's been hours. I have to be getting close. Didn't Liam say two hours by horseback? Yet that was in good weather. Still, I will do anything to prevent Michael from being hurt. Even if It means shivering through a wet, darkened forest alone for hours.

Suddenly I feel as though a covering drapes across my back. A blanket of peace. A veil of direction. I frown and look behind me, though no one follows and there's still not a sign in sight of where to go. Yet all of a sudden, it becomes clear to me as I look up higher, feeling lighter, that I'm not completely alone.

I'm not alone at all.

I let my heavy eyelids fall, lifting a prayer to the heavens I can't see but only feel, above the jumbling of sagging branches. In the rain, the thunder shouts as if desperate to be a proclamation of God's power, and I drop again to Faithful's strong neck.

"Father. I'm lost," I cry. "More than I've ever been. You are powerful, completely able. Please, God," my whisper kisses Faithful's mane, "light the way."

I lift a wavering chin, accepting that I am lost. But a new confidence works its way through me, giving me faith to keep going, though I've no idea in which direction I'm heading. Blinking tired eyes, I swipe my forehead, believing God will lead me somewhere for my best, where He wants me for whatever reason. Perhaps He'll use me to help Michael. Even as the thunder booms and lighting strikes, I remember God is the God of the storm, and lift my head to the rain as I ride.

The trees grow thicker to the right. I pause, studying the mass of limbs and blowing leaves. A branch flies in my direction without warning, flinging by my head as I duck and squeeze tight to Faithful. I quickly decide on the path to the left, rushing away from the dark thicket. Changing to a trot, I stare ahead and emerge into the slimmer part of the forest. I stop short, panting, cold fingers gripping the saddle horn and reins.

Where to go . . .

Instincts numb from the bitter chill of North Carolina's stormy winds, I wait. For anything, any sign, any sense of direction to come. But I feel utterly void of guidance.

Then, for the first time in years, Faithful begins to tug against my reins. I feel my face light in excitement as I loosen my grip, feeling the reins barely slip from my fingers as she moves.

She starts off towards the lighter thicket of trees, and I decide to let her lead. Letting go of my instincts and giving up any trust in my own abilities, I ride with a pounding heart. Lightning illuminates the forest on my side, revealing a crow hunched in black. I squint, moving on, picking up speed.

A crack sounds, near and to the side, as lighting strikes like a stick hitting a rock.

I scream, arms shaking. A shiver running down my spine to my legs, eyes darting back and forth above the soaked skin underneath. As if being chased by a black cloud, I kick Faithful with the stirrups, trusting the direction she leads, and we do not stop for what seems like nearly an hour of hard riding in the storm. Wind howls like a coyote at night, my heart pounds wildly from our frantic pace. Fire runs through my legs from holding onto Faithful with all my might. I turn to the side where I've finally come upon an opening in the forest. An open field lies ahead of me, and as the rain is slowing down to a drizzle, I'm able to see a little further. I stop Faithful, catching a breath and staring into open space. The fields are not comforting but only offer more traveling in the wet night. My head clears as I blink away rain and fearful thoughts take up residence inside, thoughts of where I could be and how many ways this night could now go wrong.

No. I won't give in to the worst of thoughts. Momma's words ring true, especially now. "Maddie, if Peter was right, then God did not give you a spirit of fear. Never give in to fearful thoughts. Think with power, love, and a sound mind, just like Peter said."

My eyelids grow heavy as I think of Momma, except a flicker of something faintly bright tells them to open. I jerk my head up, almost ready to slap my cheek to awake, and settle a watery gaze on a light not near but also not too far. My eyes focus with great strain and I nearly fall out of the saddle, leaning so far forward, intently trying to make out the image.

That . . . that can't be.

I hear the heartbeat in my chest resound in my ears. Hope flickers in my heart as a flicker of several fires light the horizon a mile ahead. My feet nudge Faithful and I pop the reins. "Let's go girl. That can only be one thing."

20

TRAITORS BY FIRELIGHT

A WARNING SHOOTS OFF in my head that this could be enemy territory. I slow down soon after speeding up, squinting to see what lies ahead. Immediately I assume the campground is the British general's present hideout, remembering Papa's scribbled, yet highly comparable drawing of many ink dots representing fires.

Stopping Faithful, I dismount, feet landing on plush fields of tall grass. I grip the reins and bring Faithful to a nearby tree on the edge of the quiet forest, wrapping the reins around the bark and giving them a tie. I calm my heart rate, swiftly making my way to the tall stands of grass that act as concealment. How close I should get to the camp, I do not know, but the Lord led me to the place I prayed for, the place to help Michael. So, I will let Him lead me as close as I can get. The rescue could not have happened already, for the camp seems quiet and no one is moving about. I stay low, almost crawling with my arms. The dirt sticks to my soaked dress, hair running through small sticks. I feel disgusting, but am also energized by the cold and the sound of swaying trees. Rain trickles and crows caw. The still camp hardly rustles with the sounds of soldiers. Thankfully the drizzle and the wind in the storm's aftermath helps conceal my movements and any sounds I make.

I frown, perplexed. Does General Ashton know we're coming? Is he hiding, waiting as a predator does just before pouncing on its prey?

I swallow, reminding myself that the general isn't expecting the colonel's daughter . . . but he also will seize me if I accidentally give away my cover. I lift my head from the grass, pulling back two threads with cold hands. I must wait, be patient and slow. My focused eyes find the thicket of several bushes nearby the outside of camp. The perfect cover. My toes curl, fingers finding the soft dirt, and I crawl again with the swooshing sound of grass sliding above my head. The bushes are not but ten yards away. Still . . . I breathe deeply, moving slowly with the wind.

Eery silence blows and moves around the ghost camp, the area lit only by several fires and a moon turned misty grey by the storm. Torches stand as the only guards to the camp, though not able to fend off any enemies also known as the American troops. Just as I'm asking myself how the torches could stay lit in this drizzle, I notice the interesting cone like covers that protect the torches from the rain. These Dragoons are crafty.

Something near and chilling travels down my spine, feeling as if someone's behind my back. Even the drizzle has stopped now and with the wind dying down, I begin to hear grass rustle right behind me. I gasp, spinning while staying low and still on my hands. The field is empty as I look down, seeing it was my dress that made the sound. Though just as quickly, a sharp crack snaps my head back to full attention, a large glow lighting in the near distance. I hold my breath, listening to a sudden chuckle and two snickers.

Glaring ahead, I sweep both hands through the grass, determined to get closer.

Quickly I see a scene equally confusing as alarming yet I move further, scrambling behind the bushes finally close enough to touch. I fall onto the ground, turning and squinting through an opening as I catch see the fire and its companions.

Two girls and a young soldier huddle closely around the orange flames, tin mugs in hands that steam with warm mist. I strain my head, urging to see around the fire between the strangers and me. Crawling to the other side of the bushes, a hand shoots to cover my mouth. Golden hair wraps around the hand of a dark eyed Dragoon as he pulls the girl to his lips, kissing her mouth forcefully. I scramble back, petrified, as Irene moves in closer to Warren's side. My breathing quickens and my vision blurs as I raise a hand to my head, rubbing both temples.

I—Irene?

How could she . . . she's . . .

A traitor!

I don't dare say it aloud for fear of being caught, but my insides burn with rage, lip curling and hands tightening around dirt. I look back to confirm that Sarah's at her side, loopy with the warmth of the fire and comfort of food and drink. Irene laughs aloud at Warren's playful gestures, Sarah watching as if glad her only heir has finally found a lad. I nearly gag over the bushes, wishing the sickening pit in my stomach would disappear.

How could they do this?

They've deliberately, delightfully, betrayed our country and my own family.

Once Papa finds out about this . . . Sarah will be imprisoned for being a traitor to the Americans, never allowed near me or Michael again!

I grit my teeth and press hard with both palms, their imprint stamping into the ground. I breathe in and out, forcing my mind to calm. There's nothing I can do about it yet.

My ears tune in to the sound of crickets, the soft crackle of the fire by Warren and the girls drawing me in. I peek around the bush again, tempted to confront them and their horrendous acts. But I let the tension fall, having already learned what anger and worry do to someone who can do nothing in the moment but only leave it to God. I couldn't do anything about Michael, but now that time has come. The same will be done for Sarah, Irene, *and* Warren.

Patience must be practiced now.

I furrow my brow, waiting like a lioness in hiding and ready to leap, except where to leap, I am not sure. I settle deeper in the dirt and restlessness stirs.

Papa and the men should be arriving any minute . . .

Suddenly, a twig snaps in the near distance ahead, unseen but reaching my ears. Unnerved, I peer around and spot it.

I spot *them*.

Liam and Kel are on the outskirts of the camp, comfortably walking in as if they belong there. Their clothes have been traded for Dragoon uniforms. They act relaxed, even joking with each other while also scanning the camp quickly to see who has noticed their arrival after the changing of the guards. I wrinkle my brow and breathe in musty air. I can't help but be excited to see how they plan on executing the rescue, but fear grips and twists my stomach at all that could go wrong. "Please, God . . ." I don't know what I'm asking for in my tiny whisper. More than I know how to word. Safety, victory, guidance. We *need* Him.

I will never doubt You again if you get Michael out of here . . . I promise.

I tighten my lips in silence, watching the men enter the camp and move toward the center of all the tents, most likely where Michael must be held. They are seconds away from carrying out the most dangerous part of the mission. My teeth grit in sudden aggravation, desperate to not just watch Michael's rescue from the side lines but take part in it. Like a soldier, someone loyal and strong. Fierce and devoted to a cause higher than herself.

The person Michael needs right now.

I take in a cold breath, rain starting up again and beginning to pelt like bullets. Looking from side to side and studying the darkened, round tents, I see Sarah and Irene quickly move inside one to escape the rain. My shoes dig into mud, ready to run. My eyes dart furiously from tent to tent, careful. Quick, focused, I slowly slip past the bushes and move closer to the edge of the camp than I should, determined to get closer. I refuse to stand by and watch. Even the soldiers, though not engaging in the mission, each have a special assignment.

Thankfully, there is a supply wagon not twenty yards from the nearest tent and I'm able to kneel behind it and still see most of the camp. My shoes slip even further into the ground as my cold fingers grip the wagon's wheel. Liam and Kel close in, faster than I was expecting, footing quick and heads turning in every direction as they continue to scan the area. I lean forwards, watching, as my skin starts to heat from anticipation and feel like fire instead of ice.

They reach a tent near the middle and stop, looking several yards ahead where a larger tent lies.

Michael.

He has to be in there. I internally yell at Liam and Kel, demanding they go, finish the mission, as they move further, one step closer...

The tent is tall and rectangular, like the Headquarters back in our own camp. Surely there is much room inside and more than one man holding Michael. Which means Liam and Kel could be heavily outgunned.

Another step.

They stand close to the entrance. Are they not seen from inside, their shadows scaling the tent's walls in dark figures? My nerves tingle in suspense. I tremble in fear of the possible outcomes.

It's gonna work, it's gonna work . . .

They move, arms extended with a short pistol in each hand. Good. Maybe they won't be outgunned after all. Liam enters first with amazing speed, hardly even whipping back the flap as he slips through. Kel follows, standing with half his body in and the other half out in order to keep an eye on the surrounding area.

I hold my breath, too scared to pray. "Please, please . . ." My mind is numb to all but this plea. Movement rustles the walls of the tent, and leaning forward, peeking out from the concealment of the forest, I hear words that sends chills down my spine.

"Where's the colonel, boy?" A dark, husky voice seems to silence every living thing close by.

General Ashton.

292

21

HANDS TO RESCUE

A GUN COCKS WITH a loud click as Liam's voice becomes hushed in the rain. I crouch, taking careful steps around the wagon, inching closer to hear.

"If the colonel wanted to see you in person, general, I believe he would have. Now it's just you and your men, and me and mine." Liam's voice is steady, even and calm as I imagine a smoothly carved pistol in each of his bronzed hands. "We have men lining the trees like a pack of wolves ready to pounce." I sense him pausing to read the bitter general's eyes, almost seeing him cock his head in his own winsome, cunning way. "If there is to be gunfire tonight, the first musket ball will most certainly find its way to your heart. But would you really favor being known as a man who desired bloodshed?" Liam's voice peaks with mystery, toying with the impatient general. "Let me take the boy and then you and Col. Holt can have your reunion at a later date, otherwise I might have to fire. And if you think I'll miss, general, please tell me . . ." I hold my breath and imagine the green spark in his eyes. "Does my hand shake?"

Then General Ashton's revengeful laugh pierces the silence and I feel like cowering underneath the canopy of the forest once more. "Young boy, you are smarter than most, I admit. But I am not intimated by you and am getting quite bored of this chatter." The general's voice hardens and I hear the crack of a hand against a hard table. "Order your regiment to surrender, or the boy dies whether you get a shot off at me or not."

Silence.

A soft, boyish whimper cuts to the very marrow of my bones.

A hard slap to Michael's cheek makes me jerk, almost sending me into the tent to liberate him myself. "Are you so deaf? I said order the surrender!"

I run over the idea of Liam pushing back again or ordering a surrender, mind racing and heart desperate. He wouldn't be so foolish to surrender, but will he be so brave to demand Michael over again?

"The boy comes with me, general. No other options." I listen for any waver in Liam's raspy voice. Finding none, a smile tugs at my cold lips. I breathe in heavily.

He can do it, he really can.

But of course, the general will not be so easily convinced.

"Son, I have a proposition, and it is the only one by which I will agree to hand over the boy. He's been quite irritating anyways, thrashing and kicking about, refusing to be quiet about how his Papa is going to kill me." I clench my fists, prouder than ever of Michael and his resilience against the British men's treatment. "You tell that colonel to come out from hiding if he wants to save any bit of his son. If not," the general's voice raises in an authoritative warning, "I'll send that boy back with half his limbs."

I bite my lip to keep the tears from running as hot coals over my cheeks. Short breaths come out as panicky whispers. "No, no, no . . ."

I asked You to get him out . . . I begged you!

"That's not an option, general." I hear the desperation in Liam's voice and I quiver in the rain's soft shower. A blanket of defeat seems to drape over all hope that remained.

The pause echoes unbearably too long.

"Not unless you care to die tonight."

Pain ripples through my chest so that I tear at my dress's material for relief, frightened now for Liam's life and not even allowing myself to consider losing he and Michael this night. A yell and then a slap, the sound of Michael trying to escape the general's grip and suffering a blow makes me cringe and lower further to the ground with a tremble.

"Michael! Don't, don't . . ." Liam's panicked command silences Michael's cry. I whimper, huddling my knees to my chest and biting my dress to keep from screaming at the entire situation.

"Boy, I'm getting tired of this. Get the colonel or we're through." The change in the general's tone makes my heart pound in an urgent desire to see Michael and Liam walk out of the tent. My eyes dart furiously at the ground, searching their options. Can Liam grab Michael and run out while Kel holds the general at gunpoint?

Not if there are several Dragoons in the tent.

The air itself seems to tense in suspense, and the long silence pierces the night as loudly as the gunshot that suddenly rips through the tents wall. A British soldier stumbles out, tearing through the material and to the ground, holding his blood-covered chest. Liam's bellow blends in with a second gunshot and a rough cry. "Michael, *run!*"

I burst forwards, standing, as I reach out to catch the heart jerking out of my chest.

Liam's entire body flies, thrown by a bullet. He slams into the side of the tent, limp as a broken bone, and slides down the canvas right before my eyes. Blood follows his trail, down the tent wall. Even from where I stand, it's easy to see his shirt turn a dark red where his ribs lie. My mind stops processing what is happening, and suddenly I cannot understand why two other shadows bend to pull up Liam's slumped form. The salty tears in my eyes blur my vision, but I see Kel hold a small frame as he charges from the tent with the desperation of an animal escaping its predator.

As if hit with a dagger, I stumble, swaying from side to side, gripping the sides of my face. "Wait, wait!" I can't stop my cry. I look from Kel to the tent in furious angst, torn apart, the shadow of Liam's limp body obvious through the tent's canvas.

"Liam, Liam . . ." I hardly even notice my own voice as I break into a run without thinking, stumbling past the tent and towards Kel. "Stop it!" My voice cracks violently, carried away by the raging wind so that he doesn't hear me. I reach him in only a second, tearing at his shirt. "Stop it, stop! Please!" My lip quivers under the weight of terror.

The alarm in Kel's face shows it all, that he will not think for one second about coming back for Liam, not while the colonel's son is in his hands. "You foolish girl! Run! Just run!"

"Kel!" I scream in sudden outrage, terrified, broken all at once at the simple thought of Liam O'Dally. My teeth grit and I grab Michael's wrist, torn between the longing to hold him and the relentless ache to see Liam alive. My hoarse shout echoes in Kel's face. "I have Michael! Get Liam back! Go!"

I see the change in Kel's face. I know he will go.

I gather Michael in my arms as his legs swing around my waist, and run. The fire in my veins hasn't completely diminished, just slightly bigger than the terrible sobs that shake my shoulders. Looking back, I strain to see any sign, any hint of Liam being alive. A groan—almost a growl—escapes through my gritting teeth as I struggle to turn my head fully behind my shoulder. "Come on, Liam . . ."

Shoes slipping in mud, I stare ahead again to keep my footing. We approach the outside of camp where the dark canopy of the forest hides, and it's here, as we slow down from the run, that I find the colonel's gaze.

Michael immediately slides out of my arms and into his. I hold my stomach, wondering how it all happened so fast. How everything went wrong. The fear in Papa's face is no match for the anger, and he looks from me to Fields and back, kissing the top of Michael's wet head and rocking him back and forth.

"I can explain everything," I hurry, urgent. "Liam's shot, Kel went back, and I took Michael." I move up next his chest, forcing him to understand with my burning eyes. "Please, Papa! We have to help."

Something snaps in his eyes. The reality of it all and the hopelessness of this night lining his brow. But deeper than this is a determination to fight.

And yet . . .

"No." His voice is cracked and pained as he hoists Michael up. "We must leave."

My hesitancy keeps my feet to the ground.

"NOW!"

I jump, fresh tears flowing. Fields nods firmly and turns, leading the way of escape into the forest. My lips fumble in response, hands gripping onto Papa's shirt. "What?" I can't stop my words laced with anger. "Papa! Go back!"

His broad back faces me and I consider turning around myself. But I can't leave Michael, not after just rescuing him. My fists clench and all I want is to pull at the back of Papa's coat, force him around, anything.

Anything . . .

"Liam! What about Liam! Papa!"

But no one hears the hopeless scream, not even the trees.

22

RIDING ON

I DUCK MY HEAD under the hanging branches, flying past forest trees as we ride with the first ray of morning light. Faithful's hooves stomp into mud, sending dirt into the air. My body moves up and down in my saddle with Michael behind me, his small hands wrapped around my waist. I blow a strand of hair out of my mouth, breathing in and out. I almost yell out for Papa to stop, ready to do anything to convince him to turn around.

Yet he still rides, Fields close by. It occurs to me that I have no idea where Tomah and Woods are. Could they have been caught too? There had to have been over one hundred soldiers in that camp. They were just asleep, in their tents, though surely they were all awakened after Liam got shot. The memory flashes before my eyes, making me wince with fresh pain. I hear the gunshot in my ears and silence a small whimper with the biting of my lip.

Faithful stumbles over branches below, making Michael and I rock in the saddle. "Hold tight." I shout over my shoulder to his curly head. I barely glance at his widened blue eyes. The poor boy. He hasn't said a word.

"Stop!" Papa's hand raises, signaling us to stop. His chestnut steed, Patriot, slows to a trot, soon to just a walk as Papa slides off the saddle. I eye him, pulse fast, swinging a leg over my saddle and hopping to the ground.

I approach him, fists clenched around my dress. "Papa, please—"

"No, Maddie." His icy eyes slice like a knife, whisper cutting through the air like a sword. Emotion glazes over his face, held back by his furrowed brow. "There was no time." He flicks his head to the side. "Bring Faithful to the creek. Get Michael a drink." He nods to Michael who stands at my side with hands gripping the side of my dress.

I look down, tossing his hair. Grabbing her reins, I lead Faithful to the running water close by with Michael at my side. My thoughts race, heart pounding as I fill our canteen and let Faithful drink. What's next? It's all up to Papa now, but how can I know what to do if he won't even speak?

Bending over, my fingers run through water as I look to the side. Papa beckons Fields over with the curt wave of his hand and speaks too far away to be heard. I look back down, twisting on the canteen's cap with a raised brow as I slide to a sitting position on the forest ground. My hands droop with weariness, legs sore from squeezing the saddle. "Michael." I glance to my right, motioning with a hand. "Come sit with me." He walks over tentatively, crossing his legs upon sitting by my side. I study him, wanting to hug him though he sits silent a foot away. Frowning, my heart thumps with hurt as I look away.

What can I say? What could comfort him? All I can think to do is pray, but no words come to mind. Rather my innermost being cries out, my spirit communing with His, begging for an answer, for rescue, for salvation. Michael's back . . . but now Liam's in the same position. Rescue required sacrifice, and Liam was willing to give himself up. My eyes shut in remorse as my head slowly shakes. I finger the material covering my chest. "Oh, Liam." My whisper hardly escapes into the crisp morning air, carried away with the quiet river. I refuse to let the tears fall.

But how they burn.

Both they and a greater pain burns within, unable to be tamed, desperate to be healed. A silent sob shakes my shoulders and I cover my face with my hands.

"Be back no later than noon. We need to lead the people to the new safe haven immediately. The Dragoons could be tracking us this moment." Papa's burdened voice lifts my head from my hands and to the side where I find him giving orders to Fields to ride into town and clear it of Dragoons.

I sniff, daring to speak aloud with my cracked voice. "Papa—it was raining hard when we left the Dragoon camp. None were awake," I quicken, rising to my feet and wiping my hair away. "I don't think they could have followed us that easily."

His shoulders lift and fall with a loud sigh as his head hangs. His eyes have seemed to sink inwards as he looks back up. "That is true. But we still can't take any chances. Continue to comfort Michael and I'll talk with you soon. We'll head out before too long." His short reply shuts my lips and turns me around to resume taking my spot on the ground. My fingers trail through rippling water once again.

As much as I will my mind not to wander, it trails, thinking about the terrible sight of Liam slouched against the wall of a tent. Even though I only saw his shadow through the tent, his blood smeared shirt and skin are all I can picture. And Kel? How did it all happen so quickly? Both are gone.

But not forever. I have to believe that.

I sit, blinking at the water and allowing the soothing sound of the river to silence my thoughts. Looking over, I find Papa walking, taking long, strenuous steps. Lowering to a spot beside me, he covers his head in his hands. A weary sigh leaves his lips. "How did you find us?"

I shift on the ground to face him fully, folding my hands on my lap and leaning forward. "I didn't mean to come after you, Papa. I slept, and when I woke, everyone had left. It was only Faithful and me." I hold back the anger in my voice. "What else was I supposed to do?"

"Follow the regiment to the new safe haven!" He snaps, flashing both eyes to mine. His hands move from side to side, gesturing to nothing but air. "Or River Springs! You could have ridden back to our people, but ride to the rescue mission? How could you have been so foolish, child!"

His words sting, but I cannot argue. Isn't he right? Wasn't I foolish? I thought I was brave, but his words tell me otherwise. "Papa . . ." I lower my eyes in shame. "I'm so sorry. I couldn't think to do anything else. I never intended to enter that camp. I assumed the rescue would already be over when I arrived. I only wanted to meet up with you on your way to River Springs." My eyes flood from the pain that took place in the Dragoon camp. "But then it all happened so fast, the general, the gun shots, Liam . . . I—I just couldn't help but grab Michael and beg Kel to go back for Liam." My lip barely trembles, threatened to give way to a quiver. "I'm sorry Papa. I know it was foolish."

A long moment of silence hangs in the air as Papa looks to Michael at my side. My brother still hasn't spoken, only gathering dirt in his hands and letting it fall through his fingers. "I'm just glad you both are safe." Worry lines Papa's brow as it furrows, deep care darkens his eyes. He breathes in and out. "Check the horse's saddles and our canteens. Make sure everything is prepared and ready. We'll leave at once when Fields returns."

I look up, arms on my knees. "Where's Tomah and Woods? I never even saw Tomah at the Dragoon camp."

Papa's eyes turn downcast. "I never saw them after the mission started. My guess is they are planning another rescue, this time for Liam. If he—" He glances away to pause, the reality of the situation heavy on his shoulders. "If he is still alive."

My gaze trails towards the river. There's nothing I can say. I rise, handling Faithful's saddle to check if the straps are tightened. After finishing with hers, I move on to Patriot's and finish with a long sigh. "All set, boy." Stroking his mane, I think of what it used to be like to ride with Papa in the open fields of North Carolina before the war. Before the French and Indian war, Papa's horse of choice was Patriot's mother. After she died, Faithful was given to me, just five years after I was born. Now, even Patriot is nearing old age but is still as spry as he's ever been. Papa pushes him hard. I smile against his cheek, whispering words of affection. Michael throws stones to my side, making them ripple across water. Not even a smile traces his lips.

After more than an hour of walking up along the creek, sitting to eat from out of our sack cloths of food, and re-filling the canteens, Fields' winded face appears from the trees, atop his steed. "Col, sir!" He swings over the saddle even as the horse trots into our barren space by the creek. His cheeks are flushed and the poor man's aged legs slightly shake when he stands. "It's clear, Sir. No Dragoons."

Papa releases a heavy sigh and light laugh, holding Fields' shoulder as I grin behind them and rise from sitting by the water. "Praise God. And what of the people?"

Fields flicks up a brow, seeming to brace for the news he's about to tell. "It doesn't look good. The people are safe for now, but they have no help. We must leave immediately."

His words sting, making me eager to arrive at home and see the people myself. Papa nods, walking to scoop Michael up. He places him in Faithful's saddle and walks to his own, hoisting himself onto Patriot with a grunt. "Get in front of Michael, Maddie. We have to go."

His urgent demand sends my feet moving, leg swinging over Faithful. I pop the reins and she jumps into a trot, following Patriot with Fields' steed close behind. "Hold on tight, Michael." I pull his hands closer around my waist.

Eyeing Papa's broad back gracefully rise and fall, I fight the agitation in my nerves at his curtness. His duty of protecting us and his intense focus on the mission at hand kept him from going back for Liam. I understand his reasons, but how could he have left him? How could he have turned away? I must trust him, but my heart aches to see Liam safe. How do I know if I'll even see him again? Could today be the last time I see him . . .

Please, God, no!

I bite down on my lip till' I taste blood, thinking of what my mother would say and remembering of the times she would say to count your dreams like you would the stars. We did, every night, after raising the covers over our chins. My dreams were endless, just as the stars, and I knew that pleased her. As I would list one after the other, she would laugh and her cheeks would turn pink in delight. And I wanted that moment to stay, still in time, forever. My biggest, brightest dream was to marry a soldier, I realize now, ducking my head under a limb. Water drips from the branch and onto my hair.

How had I forgotten after all those years?

It was hidden, tucked away. What would Mama say if I told her I've changed my mind? Would she caress my cheek, or encourage me to count another star, dream another dream, if I explained that I could never be married when a part of my heart has turned grey and cold?

We ride until the horses are unable to canter. Just over an hour of riding, Papa halts with the raise of his hand. "Shhhh." His hush silences us including the horses. I glance to the side, up to the trees and back down, handling the reins as Faithful steps backwards. My brow furrows in puzzlement, but I don't dare speak a word of question to Papa.

Twigs snap behind us and birds chirp softly to an unheard song. My hair whips behind my shoulder, eyes darting from side to side.

Could the Dragoons have followed us so quickly?

I move worried eyes to Papa. He signals to move. I nod, giving Faithful a kick.

We ride for half an hour more, never looking back. As we approach an opening in the forest, Papa stops and signals for me to come up beside him. His blue eyes lock on mine as I pull Faithful up. "You know this area well. I'll take Michael and watch the rear. You and Fields ride as fast as you can and gather the towns people together as soon as you arrive in town." He hoists Michael over to his own saddle.

I lick my lips eagerly, patting Faithful's neck. I bend down to whisper in her ear. "Just you and me, girl. We can ride like the wind again." I see the fire in Faithful's eye that mirrors the one in mine, her neck turned towards me, head bobbing as if to say she agrees. I can lead us now, the chilly air pushing me on. I catch up to Fields and ride past him with speed. Faithful smells my zeal and rides harder without my nudging. I smile, wind taking my auburn hair and wrapping it around my chin as we ride up-wind. So near to home, I kick Faithful on with my ankles, and she gladly obeys. I hear Papa's loud shout from the back of our group.

"Maddie! Wait for Fields!"

And, how can I? Home is so close I can smell the change in the air. It forces me on as I freely allow it to. Approaching an exit to the forest, I take it without another thought, encountering a rising hill as Faithful digs in for the climb. "Yah! Go!" I slap her sides, feeding the fire in my veins.

My eyes graze the grassy hill turned grey by the barely morning light, body bent over Faithful's creamy neck. "Come on, girl." We start up the hill, riding through clouds of fog as if on a misty mountain. Sweat drips from both mine and Faithful's brow, and I feel the urge in her to reach the top as much as it burns in me. The tops grow bigger, soon under our feet. I look behind my shoulder, eyeing Papa and Fields start up the small hill.

Looking back towards town, I brush a strand of hair away, and my stomach drops.

River Springs is desolate, darkened under the shadows the trees surrounding create. A puff of wind throws my hair back as I turn my head both ways, squinting. The air is cold, dry, alone. Not a figure is in sight down where the destroyed shops, signs, and wagons lie in heaps. Dust whirls, playing around broken pieces of what once was.

What once was my home, my everything, my playground and also my practice grounds for shooting and riding. I shake my head, tightening the reins so Faithful stays on the hill's top. Hooves stomp and come up beside me.

"Dear God . . ." Papa's voice lowers from seeing the empty land and the gloomy state of the town. With no people in sight, Papa question's Fields' earlier observation. "Are you sure the people are still here?" He turns to the veteran soldier.

Fields nods. "Yes, Sir. There were only a few actually awake when I got information."

"And you're confident we're clear?"

"We're clear."

I glance back just long enough to look to Fields and search for some sign of surety. He's sure alright, ready to trot downwards and towards the helpless people looking for a new safe haven.

I don't wait for new orders, Papa already told me to ride as fast as I can. If Fields has trouble keeping up, well, he'll get there eventually. I start the ride down, the rest following behind. With each step, an eery silence echoes in my ears. I swallow, licking my dry lips, nudging Faithful on, but even she seems hesitant to get closer herself. "It's okay, girl." I speak the words of comfort more for myself than her, unwilling to confront the twisted pit in my stomach.

What is this? This alarm and fear gripping my insides? There are no Dragoons, Fields confirmed it. So what do I have to fear? What I will find up and down the streets?

Behold, I am with you, to the very end of the age.

I slap the reins, listening to His voice.

Jesus promised.

He's with me. He's with me.

I ride on, this time harder, and reach the bottom of the hill where broken pieces lie.

23

NEW MERCIES

I BEND TO A KNEE, letting dirt fall through my fingers. Covered in dust is every inch of my hometown. Looking up, I study the shops. *Annie's* still stands, though the entire left side has fallen.

I rise, wiping my hands, walking up the wooden steps I once skipped to get a stick of chocolate.

"Maddie, you know she loves you," she tried to convince me of Sarah as she leaned on the counter, hazel eyes reading every part of mine as if she was my own mother. My eyes burn, threatened by tears of regret.

I walk into the shop, coughing away dust, finding pieces of candy littered across the broken floors. The shop used to be beautiful, now down to only half a wall and some steps. "Oh, Miss Annie . . ." I finger the paper covering some candies, lowering to the floors. My eyes sweep over the room. "I'm so sorry."

A loud commotion sounds from outside the shop as I rise and walk. Looking out the door, I find the faces of people of River Springs who have begun to gather once they had seen that they have visitors. I step out slowly, frowning, each step creaking as I walk down. The few people who are awake suddenly yell and jab insults, unable to discuss what to do about people riding upon town.

I hurry, approaching with swift feet.

"Please, do not fight." My compassionate eyes sweep over the tired faces. They recognize me as the colonel's daughter almost immediately. The man to my right, a bushy red head with intense blue eyes, points a finger with a lit grin.

"Maddie! What are you doing here?"

"Where's the colonel?"

"Are those nasty redcoats coming back?"

The rest gasp and spit curses at the last comment. I flinch, hurting at the state of our people who obviously do not know what else to do besides quarrel. Anxiously, I glance behind my shoulder, finding him approaching the bottom of the hill. "Look . . ." I turn back, finding their scared eyes. "My father is coming. We're taking you to a safe haven immediately. You all need to gather your things. Where are the rest of the townspeople?"

One woman shakes her head tiredly, almost unwilling to respond. "They all would rather stay inside the shops where they have set up shelter. They're too scared to go back to their homes."

Sadness pricks my heart. It all came down so fast, and they had no time to prepare.

No matter. We must move now.

I raise my voice a little louder, gathering every ounce of courage left in me as the people shuffle. "Go, warn the rest of the people. We must leave for the safe haven immediately." I pause, watching their feet planted to the ground in confusion. My eyes widen, lips parting. "Do you want to be here when the redcoats return? Please, hurry!"

The small group moves hurriedly, spreading out to the various shops where others have holed up. I walk back to the bottom of the hill to meet the men as the sun rises higher and light peeks through the trees. Papa hops down, taking Michael off the saddle as Fields jumps to the ground beside them. "They said the rest of the people have been hiding since the attack." I furrow my brow in displeasure, ashamed of my people's cowardice yet sympathetic to their fear. "What are my orders, Papa?" I look up to his focused blue gaze sweeping over the emptiness of town.

"Bring the horses to town, tie them up and gather the people." His eyes flicker to mine in a moment of fierce determination that mirrors my own as he walks past my shoulder, head up, strides strong.

I grab the reins to Patriot and Faithful and lead them forward. Michael falls in step by me, clenching the material of my dress. Pulling his head into my side, I narrow a darkened gaze on the streets of town, targeting one shop after tying up the horses.

The boards creak under my feet with every step, wind whistling through the cracks and crevices. Peeking through, I search the small room inside the boutique with hesitant eyes. I almost call out until I see heads raise from behind broken counters. Releasing Michael, I hold my breath, stepping forward. "Please, come outside. The colonel is back from war and is here to take us to a safe haven."

Fearfully, several heads pop up along with tired bodies, and an older woman with gray hair steps forward as she smooths down her brown dress. "My dear, you are an answer to prayer. Where is your father?" She looks about, then back behind her shoulder at the rest of the hiding citizens. "Take courage, my friends. We are safe now. The Lord is on our side."

I admire the woman, nodding quickly to the rest. "Follow me."

The rest emerge from the building like flocks of sheep, at least twenty coming out of hiding and ducking their heads upon exiting. I step backwards, my skips turning carefree and my smile light. "Do not be afraid. You are all alright now." A small woman smiles in the back, catching my eye. I spin, jogging with Michael in hand to the next shop, giving the same report to the people inside. "Gather all you have, especially any weapons and food, meet outside in front of Annie's."

At least one hundred have gathered together by the end of half an hour. Papa looks to the group and nods confidently. I can't help but grin, grateful. As Papa counts the heads, I begin to turn. Brushing hair away from my eyes, my glance stops on a small house on the outskirts of town, its door wide open and chimney cold and empty.

Something constricts in my throat as I step forward. Michael's hand slips out from my own. The house is dark and cold. I can tell even from so many yards away. I squint, titling my head in a light cock and picking up my pace. The familiarity beckons me, and I can almost hear Sarah's demanding screams and Michael's bubbling laughter, his scuffling boots, if I listen close enough and close my eyes. The windows are shattered. My steps become silent as they sweep through dead grass, eyes falling on the house now just in front of me. It's so close that I reach out several fingers to trace the dark, dying wood, and my breath becomes chilly as I breathe out, leaning my forehead against the rough outside wall.

How many times have I smiled in this house? Cried in Papa's arms . . . dreamed in Mama's?

I let the tears fall from my cheeks and wet the dry grass. A whimper shakes my shoulders as it quietly escapes my lips. The air is musty, itching at my nose as I swipe my eyes and step through. Tables are overturned and the cupboard where I once retrieved my tea cup is torn out from the wall. The floor's splintered wood lies underneath cracked cups and plates.

My head moves in slow, soft shakes, feet planted. To take Michael and do this to the house, my beloved home which has been the recipient of so many memories . . . the Royal Dragoons are heartless. Cold. My feet crunch above broken glass. As if the air is whispering, I hear her still.

"You're too young to understand, child . . ."

I shake, whipping to the side and watching the exchange.

"*You see, the mother I was raised by actually taught me a little something about dignity.*" I watched the color leave her face, the anger boil in her veins. And yet she couldn't respond as I plucked the toy soldier from her grip. "*I made that money with my own hours,*" my pained voice echoes in my ears, off the cabin walls, to the ground below. "*That's more than you'll ever do for this family.*"

I look down to my feet, the air cold again. How was that not long ago, less than a week, when it seems like an eternity? I look back to the door, where a broken girl in her tattered dress stormed out, afraid and confused.

Has that girl changed at all?

I take light steps to the back room, ignoring the eery sound of boards creeping under my aging leather boots. I hold the edge of an emerging wall, entering the hallway leading to our bedrooms. Sarah's room sits on the far right, in the back. I take the turn, walking to and opening her door. The air inside seems even more dusty and cold than the rest of the house. As if death lingers around the corner, I hesitantly enter, hugging my sides, and eye the chest in front of Sarah's bed. My brow furrows in, heart pounding. I've never looked inside it, but now I'm drawn, as if thinking somehow in the chest I will find the secrets to her strange behavior. I walk and bend to the chest and finger it's lid. Opening with a quiet swing, I find a single letter atop pieces of clothing. The color of its brown paper stands out against the cream-colored material beneath it, and I reach for it like it's a magnet. In my hands, the letter feels like sandpaper as I unfold its creased edges.

"Mrs. Haverd..."

"Haverd?" I question aloud.

What in the world?

I read on, eyes darting from line to line anxiously. A dark chill works down my spine as I walk back towards the front of the house, clenching the paper in hand. The first words are enough to stop me in my tracks.

"*Your reports are helpful. But information is scarce. The nights are becoming unbearable with the thought of Colonel John Holt still having breath in his lungs.*

We will fix that, won't we? Soon. But I need your help. I need more of it. You give me what I've required, and I'll give you a life you can only imagine. Marriage into the highest of society, wealth, status, it will all be yours. But first you must do your part. Gather the information of John's current position and the state of his regiment, and you will soon have the deserved love of a man that the colonel has never given.

Be quick, be lethal. —Dominick Ashton."

My head spins as the floor rocks beneath me. I stumble to the front door, leaning against its frame while looking out towards town.

The people are rallying around Papa, ignited by the hope of a new haven. My breathing becomes quick, nausea twisting my insides. I clench my stomach, desperate for escape.

Papa. I must get this to Papa!

My wants to scream. The traitors! They ruined everything, they freely handed Papa and my family over to the hands of evil, murderous men. And yet they're called Americans!

I bite my cheek, looking quickly over the letter again. General Ashton was paying Sarah for information with the promise of marriage?

I cover my mouth, sickened.

It can't be, it just can't.

Oh, Papa . . .

How hated he is by this man. And whatever did he do to deserve such hate? I know only half the story, which involves Mama, but it certainly does not warrant such cruelty from one man.

I close my eyes, not willing to read it again, desperate to burn it, throw it, anything.

Their voices outside reach my ears. Shouts of hope and more. I look out and watch them hug, clenching the paper. They laugh with the promise of safety, the expected journey ahead to Green Mountain. Smiling, every one of them breathes out relief and yet waits in anticipation to hear Papa's next words.

His back straightens, and his stays lit with strong confidence. Pushing away from the doorframe, I can hear his clear and deep voice ring out among empty spaces and into the hearts of each person gathered.

"We have a hope greater than ourselves." He points, lifting both eyes to the lightened skies. "Look up. Always look up, and you will no longer fear what is below." His smile is sure, so generous and warm. He pauses until meeting the eyes of each citizen. I'm now close enough to hear him as his voice drops. I keep walking towards the group as leaves crunch beneath my shoes, unable to give a smile even though the sun is starting to rise higher. "We will arrive late tonight, so prepare for a long journey. Pack all the food you can," Papa nods, looking upon their weary faces, "bring all the water you can get, and wrap up. It will be cold on these mountains."

The people seem to pale at the mention of climbing North Carolina's vast mountains, but the hopeful spark in Papa's eyes is a light in the dark. It will carry them on, keeping them awake with faith, fueled with belief.

"Do not be discouraged. We have mercy on our side. He is gracious and the way has already been prepared." Something changes in his tough face, a warning to the people. "It won't be easy, friends. That's a guarantee. But during the climb, we can trust the words of James, who told us to count it all joy when we experience tough trials." His face lights with a grin, growing with the rising sun. "A new day is dawning, friends. This time tomorrow we will awaken to new beginnings."

I grasp the letter in hand, drooping my eyelids. The grass sweeps over my boots as I walk closer, now only ten yards away. The distress is still yet evident in the people's faces as I approach, heartache showing in hunched shoulders. Slowly I slide the letter into my pocket, walking on as anxiety still grapples at my heart. Yet I'm suddenly reminded of the Psalm that says His mercies are new every morning.

Isn't it like Papa said? Don't we have mercy on our side, a hope greater than ourselves?

I try to breathe out the angst almost choking out all peace and nod to the lady on my left. Studying her eyes, I notice that they are on fire compared to the others. It seems that slowly, like spring thawing away winter's remnants, it fans the flames in my own gaze, and I find a way to nod with her.

I'm a Holt. I must inspire, and I must encourage. I stuff the letter away, deciding there will be time later to show Papa. My feet begin to quicken under long strides, heart starting to beat with a growing passion for freedom, and with a hope for independence. Stepping close to Papa, I realize that I glide on God's mercies like riding dawn. My eyes sweep over the people, and I hear her words.

"A purpose . . ."

Huddled under the covers of my bed, I peered into gentle eyes of brown and felt something kindle inside as she encouraged the small spark to fan into a flame.

"We each have one. Pursue yours, Maddie."

I now hear my mother's command like the pounding of my heart beating in my ears. Strong, steady, alive.

"It's calling you."

I nod under the glare of burning light and straighten next to Papa, the sun just now risen and hanging high above the tree line. Ignited by Who lives within me, I know full well that I can do all things through Him.

For if God is for us, who can be against us?

The lady who emerged from the shop earlier walks up as she clenches her brown dress. "You are the patriot's daughter, aren't you?" Her eyes are different this time, aglow and big as she nods to the colonel at our side.

"The patriot's daughter?" I smile, looking to Papa and back. "Yes, Miss. But . . ." She reads my eyes as I pause to consider my words, and I feel my back straighten as I speak. "I am not just the daughter of a patriot." Biting my lip, I look above Papa, above their faces and into the light, where hope lies.

I find the lady's eyes and hide a grin. "I am one."

LEARN TO DEFEND YOUR FAMILY & YOUR FREEDOM!

Join the Green Family for a combination of Constitution Training from Rick and Handgun Defense Training from some of the top instructors in the Nation. To order DVD's of Constitutional Defense or for more information on attending a live class, visit RickGreen.com.

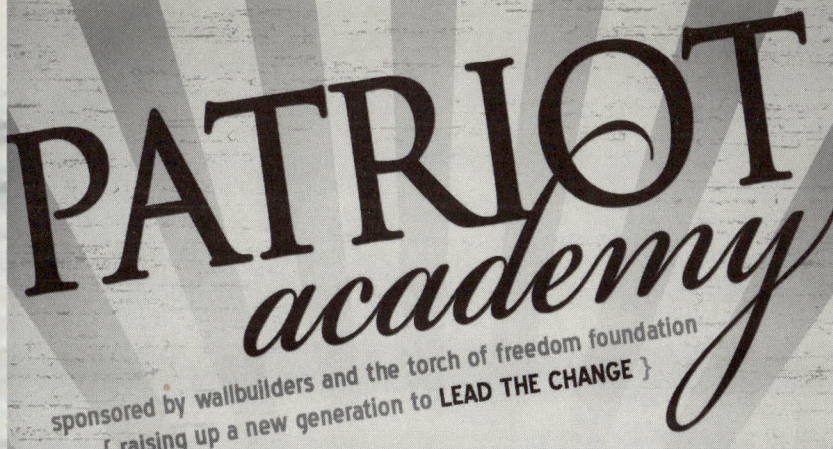

PATRIOT academy

sponsored by wallbuilders and the torch of freedom foundation
{ raising up a new generation to **LEAD THE CHANGE** }

CHALLENGE YOUR IDEA OF GOVERNMENT

At Patriot Academy, you don't just learn about government, you live it. This summer, you and your fellow students, ages 16-25, will take over the Texas state government at the Capitol Building in Austin, Texas. You will work together to form a fully functioning mock government, drafting legislation, running committee meetings, debating bills, electing leaders and passing laws.

CONFRONT THE ISSUES OF TODAY

In a fast-paced, interactive format, elected officials and experts will explain today's most relevant issues. Through media relations training, public speaking workshops and spirited debate, you will learn to articulate what you believe and why. Patriot Academy will equip you to effect change for the issues that matter most to you, whether as a concerned citizen or political candidate.

CHAMPION THE CAUSE OF FREEDOM

If you want to be a part of a new generation of young leaders poised to change the future of American politics, join us at Patriot Academy. You won't want to miss it!

FOR MORE INFORMATION OR TO APPLY, VISIT US AT
WWW.PATRIOTACADEMY.COM

BRING
Wallbuilder's LIVE *host*,
RICK GREEN's

Constitution Alive!

to YOUR area

History and government do NOT have to be boring! Rick Green brings the Constitution and citizenship to life through compelling, entertaining, and even funny stories about the lives, fortunes, and sacred honor sacrificed to make America the most powerful, most free nation in the history of the world.

> "I have never heard a more down-to-earth, common sense version of our Constitution and what it was intended to do than the one given by Rick Green." -Joni C., TX

> "Having Rick speak to us about our nation's history was truly a blessing. Not only did he impart historical facts, he gave us direction and motivation to stay in the battle for our country." -Lyleann T., TX

> "We have been looking for a class just like this for years! It is concise, engaging, interesting, and ties in our Biblical foundations. Just the right balance of studying the actual text, historical context and current events." -Lori G., WA

"The seminar was gripping, informative, and impacting! It was so great to be properly informed on what our nation was really founded on and our rights as citizens of the U.S. Each person who attended left with a lasting impression and gained fresh insight about our nation. The Constitution Seminar was a great tool for our church and we are excited to see the fruit that comes from each person who attended." -Pastor Mark

Schedule your class now and let's help restore America back to her Founding Principles!

One of the most dynamic & inspirational speakers in America today, nationally known Constitutional teacher, and co-host of the national radio program "WallBuilders Live!" with David Barton, heard on more than 200 stations across America:

Rick Green

"Inspiring and equipping citizens to preserve liberty"

BRAD STINE & RICK GREEN PRESENT:
COMEDY AND THE CONSTITUTION

Brad Stine   Rick Green

Laugh & Learn with Brad Stine ("God's Comic") and Rick Green (WallBuilders speaker & radio host, founder of Patriot Academy) as they use hilarious history to bring America's founding documents to life.

Freedom is not a boring subject... especially when comedian Brad Stine is in the mix! This one of a kind approach to history will leave a lasting impression on your congregation and move them to action as they live out their freedom with a Biblical Worldview.

www.ConstitutionComedy.com

Have you ever wondered how legends came into being? Have you ever desired to learn from the legends of history? Have you ever desired to become a legend? 12 authors bring you stories of courage, mentorship & virtue through *Legends of Liberty*!

Legends of Liberty tells the story of 15 legends throughout history and teaches the reader how to emulate their actions in modern society. Each chapter is written by a different author, each a modern day legend in their own right.

Legends of Liberty is edited, compiled, and formulated by Rick Green. Contributing authors include David Barton, Gary Newell, Cliff Graham, Krish Dhanam, Timothy Barton, Brad Stine, Paul Tsika, Alexandra Murphy, and many others!

Legends and stories told include John Locke, King David, Nathan Hale, Squanto, Zig Zigler, Sybil Ludington, Brian Birdwell, Jimmy Robertson, Divey Langston, Moe Berg, and many others!

ABOUT THE AUTHORS...

Kamryn & Rick enjoy tag-teaming as a father/daughter speaking duo, inspiring audiences to live like patriots and preserve freedom for future generations. Rick is a former Texas State Representative, attorney, author, and nationally recognized speaker on the Constitution and America's founding principles. He currently co-hosts the daily radio talk show *WallBuilders Live! w/David Barton*. The Green Family travels the Nation together bringing history to life with their fun and entertaining live presentations, as well as their adventures in the *Chasing American Legends* reality television series.

Connect with the Green family at RickGreen.com for regular updates, articles, and liberty inspiring information!